AT RISK

Also by Patricia Cornwell

AT RISK

PATRICIA CORNWELL

DOUBLEDAY LARGE PRINT HOME LIBRARY EDITION

G. P. PUTNAM'S SONS
NEW YORK

This Large Print Edition, prepared especially for Doubleday Large Print Home Library, contains the complete, unabridged text of the original Publisher's Edition.

G.P. PUTNAM'S SONS
Publisher's Since 1838
Published by the Penguin Group
Penguin Group (USA) Inc., 375 Hudson Street, New York, New York 10014, USA • Penguin Group (Canada), 90 Eglinton Avenue East, Suite 700 Toronto, Ontario M4P 2Y3, Canada (a division of Pearson Penguin Inc.) • Penguin Books Ltd, 80 Strand, London WC2R 0RL, England • Penguin Ireland, 25 St Stephen's Green, Dublin 2, Ireland (a division of Penguin Books Ltd) • Penguin Group (Australia), 250 Camberwell Road, Camberwell, Victoria 3124, Australia (a division of Pearson Australia Group Pty Ltd) • Penguin Books India Pvt Ltd, 11 Community Centre, Panchsheel Park, New Delhi–110 017, India • Penguin Group (NZ), Cnr Airborne and Rosedale Roads, Albany Auckland 1310, New Zealand (a division of Pearson New Zealand Ltd) • Penguin Books (South Africa) (Pty) Ltd, 24 Sturdee Avenue, Rosebank, Johannesburg 2196, South Africa

Penguin Books Ltd, Registered Offices: 80 Strand, London WC2R 0RL, England

This book was originally published in serial form in *The New York Times Magazine.*

ISBN 13: 978-0-7394-6828-9
ISBN 10: 0-7394-6828-6

Printed in the United States of America

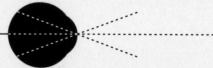

This Large Print Book carries the
Seal of Approval of N.A.V.H.

*To
Dr. Joel J. Kassimir,
a true artist*

AT RISK

An autumn storm has pounded Cambridge all day and is set to play a violent encore into the night. Lightning sears and thunder startles as Winston Garano ("Win" or "Geronimo" most people call him) strides through the dusk along the eastern border of Harvard Yard.

He has no umbrella. He has no jacket. His Hugo Boss suit and dark hair are dripping wet and pressed flat against him, his Prada shoes soaked and filthy from a false step out of the taxi into a puddle. Of course, the damn taxi driver let him out at the wrong damn address, not at 20 Quincy Street in front of the Harvard Faculty Club but at the Fogg Art Museum, and that was Win's miscalculation, really. When he got into the taxi at Logan International Airport, he happened to tell the driver, *Harvard Faculty Club, it's near the Fogg,* thought maybe if he referenced both he might sound like someone who went to Harvard or collects fine art instead of what he is, an investigator with the Massachusetts State Police who applied to Harvard seventeen years ago and didn't get in.

Big raindrops feel like irritable fingers tapping the top of his head and he is overcome by anxiety as he stands on the old red-brick walk in the midst of the old red-brick Yard, looking up and down Quincy Street, watching people spew past in cars and on bicycles, a few on foot and hunched under umbrellas. Privileged people move through the rain and mist, belonging here and knowing they do and where they are going.

"Excuse me," Win says to a guy in a black windbreaker and baggy, faded jeans. "Your Mensa question for the day."

"Huh?" He scowls, having just crossed the wet one-way street, a soggy satchel dripping from his back.

"Where's the faculty club?"

"Right there," he replies with unnecessary snottiness, probably because if Win were a faculty member or anyone important, obviously he would know where the faculty club is.

He heads toward a handsome Georgian Revival building with a gray slate roof, the brick patio blossoming with wet, white umbrellas. Lighted windows are warm in the gathering darkness, and the quiet splashing of a fountain blends with the sounds of the rain as he follows slick cobblestones to the front door, running his fingers through his wet hair. Inside, he looks around as if he's just entered a crime scene, taking in his surroundings, making judgments about what must have been a parlor for some wealthy aristocrat more than a century ago. He surveys mahogany paneling, Persian rugs, brass chandeliers, Victorian theater broadsheets, oil portraits and polished old stairs that lead somewhere he'll probably never go.

He takes a seat on a stiff antique sofa, a grandfather clock reminding him that he is exactly on time and that District Attorney Monique Lamont ("Money LaMount," as he calls her), the woman who basically runs his life, is nowhere in sight. In Massachusetts, the DAs have jurisdiction over all homicides and have their own state police investigative service assigned to them, and what that means is that Lamont can bring anybody she wants into her personal squad, meaning she can also get rid of anybody she wants. He belongs to her and she has her ways of reminding him of that.

This is the latest, the worst of all her political maneuvering, and in some instances shortsighted reasoning, or what he sometimes views as her fantasies, all of it radiating from her insatiable ambition and need to control. She suddenly decides to send him way down South to Knoxville, Tennessee, to attend the National Forensic Academy, saying that when he returns he will enlighten his colleagues about the latest innovations in crime scene investigation, show them how to do it right, exactly right. Show them how to ensure that no criminal investigation *will ever, and I mean ever, be compromised by the mishandling of evidence or the absence of procedures and analyses that should have been done,* she said. He doesn't understand it. The Massachusetts State Police has CSIs. Why not send one of them? She wouldn't listen. She wouldn't explain.

Win looks down at the soggy shoes he bought for twenty-two dollars at the vintage clothing shop called Hand-Me-Ups. He notices the beginning of dried water spots on the gray suit he got for a hundred and twenty dollars at the same shop where he's gotten quite a lot of designer clothing dirt cheap because everything is used, cast off by rich people who easily tire of things or are infirm or dead. He waits and worries, wondering what is so important that Lamont has summoned him all the way up here from Knoxville. Roy, her wimpish, supercilious press secretary, called him this morning, yanked him out of class, told him to be on the next flight to Boston.

Right this minute? Why? Win protested.
Because she said so, Roy replied.

Inside the high-rise, precast Cambridge District Court building, Monique Lamont emerges from the private powder room inside her large private office. Unlike many DAs and others who wade in the world of criminal justice, she doesn't collect police caps and patches or foreign uniforms and weapons or framed photographs of famed law enforcement officials. Those who give her such mementos do so only once, because she doesn't hesitate to give them back or away. She happens to like glass.

Art glass, stained glass, Venetian glass, new glass, old glass. When sunlight fills her office, it turns into a prismatic fire, flashing, winking, glowing, sparkling in a spectrum of colors, distracting people, amazing them. She welcomes distracted, amazed people to her rainbow, then introduces them to the nasty storm that preceded it.

"Hell no," she picks up where she left off as she sits down at her expansive glass desk, a see-through desk that doesn't deter her in the least from wearing short skirts. "Another damn educational video on drunk driving is not going to happen. Does anybody besides me think outside the box?"

"Last week in Tewksbury, an entire family was killed by a drunk driver," Roy says from a sofa catty-corner to the desk, looking at her legs when he assumes she doesn't notice. "That's far more relevant to citizens than some old murder case from some provincial Southern city nobody around here cares . . ."

"Roy." Lamont crosses her legs and watches him watching her. "Do you have a mother?"

"Come on, Monique."

"Of course you have a mother." She gets up, starts pacing, wishes the sun was out.

She hates rain.

"How would you like it, Roy, if your ninety-pound elderly mother were beaten savagely in her own home and left to die alone?"

"Oh come on, Monique. That's not the point. We should be focusing on a Massachusetts unsolved homicide, not one in Hickville. How many times do we have to go through this?"

"You're foolish, Roy. We send in one of our finest and solve it and get—"

"I know, I know. Huge national attention."

"The sure, strong hand reaching down to help those less fortunate, less, well . . . less everything. We get the old evidence, reexamine it—"

"And make Huber look good. Somehow, it will be him and the governor who look good. You're kidding yourself if you think otherwise."

"It will make *me* look good. And you're going to make sure of that—"

She abruptly stops talking as the office door opens and coincidentally, maybe too coincidentally, her law clerk walks in without knocking. Huber's son. It briefly crosses her mind that he's been eavesdropping. But the door is shut. It isn't possible.

"Toby?" she warns. "Am I psychotic or did you just walk in without knocking again?"

"Sorry about that. Man, I got too much on my mind." He sniffs, shakes his shaved head, looks half stoned. "I just wanted to remind you I'm taking off."

For good, she wishes. "I'm completely aware," she says.

"Be back next Monday. Hanging out at the Vineyard, chilling, my dad knows where to find me if you need me."

"You've taken care of all pending matters?"

He sniffs again. Lamont's pretty sure he's fond of cocaine. "Uh, like what?"

"Uh, like everything I've put on your desk," she says, tapping a gold pen on a legal pad.

"Oh, yeah, sure. And I was a good boy, cleaned up everything, straightened up so you won't have to pick up after me." He smirks, his resentful feelings toward her peeking through his fog, leaves, shuts the door.

"One of my bigger mistakes," she says. "Never do a favor for a colleague."

"It's obvious you've made your decision and it's as final as death," Roy picks up where he left off. "And I reiterate my belief that you're making a very big mistake. Maybe a fatal one."

"Cut the death analogies, Roy. They really annoy me. I could use a coffee."

Governor Miles Crawley sits in the backseat of his black limousine, the partition up, his executive protection out of sight, unable to hear him on the phone.

"Don't be so damn sure you get careless," he says, staring down at his long, pinstripe-clad legs stretched out, staring blankly at his shiny black shoes. "What if someone talks? And we shouldn't be talking about this. . . ."

"The someone involved isn't going to talk. That's guaranteed. And I'm never careless."

"No guarantees except death and taxes," the governor says, cryptically.

"In this instance, you've got a guarantee, no way to lose. Who didn't know where it was? Who lost it? Who hid it? No matter what, who looks bad?"

The governor gazes out the window at the darkness, the rain, the lights of Cambridge shining through, not so sure he should have gone along with this, decides, "Well, there's no turning back since it's out to the press. You'd damn well better hope you're right, because the person I'll blame is you. It was your damn idea."

"Trust me, it will all be good news for you."

The governor could use a little good news. His wife is a real pain in the ass these days, his bowels are acting up, and he's off to another dinner. This one is at the Fogg Art Museum, where he'll walk around looking at Degas paintings, then say a few words to make sure all the art-loving philanthropists and Harvard elitists are reminded of what a cultured man he is.

"I don't want to talk about this any further," the governor says.

"Miles . . ."

He hates being called by his first name, no matter how long he has known the person. It's *Governor Crawley.* Someday *Senator Crawley.*

". . . you'll be thanking me, I promise . . ."

"Don't make me repeat myself," Governor Crawley warns. "This is the last time we have this conversation." He ends the call, tucks his cell phone back in his jacket pocket.

The limousine pulls up to the front of the Fogg. Crawley waits for his private protection to let him out, lead him on to his next political performance, alone. Damn his wife and her damn sinus headaches. He was briefed on Degas not even an hour ago, at least knows how to pronounce his name and that he was French.

Lamont gets up, slowly paces, looking out the window at a depressingly dark, wet dusk, sipping coffee that tastes burned.

"The media's already started calling," Roy says as a warning.

"I believe that was the plan," she says.

"And we need a damage-control plan. . . ."

"Roy. I can't hear much more of this!"

He's such a coward, the gutless wonder, she thinks, her back to him.

"Monique, I just don't see how you can possibly believe that any scheme of the governor's is going to benefit you in the end."

"If we're going to get fifty million dollars to build a new crime lab," she repeats herself slowly, as if he is stupid, "we have to get attention, show the public, the legislators, we're completely justified in upgrading technology, hiring more scientists, buying more lab equipment, building the biggest DNA database in the country, maybe even in the world. We solve some old case that people in the good ol' South have left in a cardboard box for twenty years, and we're heroes. The taxpayers support us. Nothing succeeds like success."

"More of Huber's brainwashing. What crime lab director wouldn't want to talk you into that, despite the risk to you?"

"Why can't you see what a good idea this is?" she says in frustration, looking out at the rain, the relentless, dreary rain.

"Because Governor Crawley hates you," Roy replies flatly. "Ask yourself why he would hand this off to you."

"Because I'm the most visible DA in the commonwealth. I'm a woman. So he doesn't look like the small-minded, sexist, right-wing bigot he really is."

"And running against him—any failure will be on your head, not his. You'll be Robert E. Lee surrendering your sword, not him. . . ."

"So now he's Ulysses S. Grant. Win will get this done."

"More likely do you in."

She slowly turns around, faces Roy, watches him flip through a notebook.

"Just how much do you know about him?" he says.

"He's the best investigator in the unit. Politically, a perfect choice."

"Vain, obsessed with clothes." He reads his notes. "Designer suits, a Hummer, a Harley, raising questions about his finances. A Rolex."

"A Breitling. Titanium. Probably *gently used,* from one of his many secondhand shops," she says.

Roy looks up, baffled. "How do you know where he gets his stuff?"

"Because I recognize the finer things in life. One morning I asked him how he afforded the Hermès tie he happened to be wearing that day."

"Consistently late when called to crime scenes," Roy goes on.

"According to whom?"

He flips several more pages, runs down one of them with his finger. She waits for his lips to move as he silently reads. *There, they just moved. Dear God. The world is full of imbeciles.*

"Doesn't appear he's gay," Roy continues. "That's good news."

"Actually, it would be rather huge-minded of us if our poster-boy detective was gay. What does he drink?"

"Well he's not gay, that's for sure," Roy says. "A womanizer."

"According to whom? What does he like to drink?"

Roy pauses, confounded, says, "Drink? No, he doesn't have that problem at least. . . ."

"Vodka, gin, beer?" She's about to lose her patience entirely.

"I got no friggin' idea."

"Then you call his pal Huber and find out. And I mean before I get to the faculty club."

"Sometimes I just don't understand you, Monique." He returns to his notes. "Narcissistic."

"Who wouldn't be if he looked like him," she says.

"Conceited, a pretty-boy empty suit. You should hear what the other cops have to say about him."

"I believe I just did."

Win Garano enters her mind. His dark, wavy hair, flawless face. A body that looks sculpted of creamy tan stone. And his eyes, something about his eyes. When he looks at her, she gets the uncanny sensation that he is reading her, knows her, maybe even knows something she doesn't.

He'll be perfect on TV, perfect in photo shoots.

". . . probably the only two good things I can say about him is he shows well," poor inadequate Roy is saying, "and has somewhat of a minority status. Albeit high-yellow, neither nor."

"What did you just say?" Lamont stares at him. "I'm going to pretend you didn't."

"Then what do we call it?"

"We don't call it anything."

"African-Italian? Well, I guess so," he answers his own questions as he skips through the notebook. "Father was black, mother Italian. Apparently decided to give him his mother's name, Garano, for obvious reasons. Both parents dead. Faulty heater. Some dump they lived in when he was a kid."

Lamont fetches her coat from the back of the door.

"His upbringing's a mystery. Got no idea who raised him, lists no closest next of kin, the person to contact in an emergency some-one named Farouk, apparently his landlord."

She digs her car keys out of her bag.

"Less about him, more about me," she says. "His history isn't important. Mine is. My accomplishments. My record. My stand on the issues that matter. Crime. Not just today's crime. Not just yesterday's crime." She walks out the door. "Any crime, any time."

"Yup," Roy follows her. "Some campaign slogan you got there."

2

Lamont snaps shut her umbrella and unbuttons her long, black raincoat as she notices Win on an antique sofa that's about as comfortable as a wooden plank.

"Hope you haven't been waiting long," she apologizes.

If she cared about inconveniencing him, she wouldn't have ordered him to fly all the way here for dinner, interrupted his training at the National Forensic Academy, interrupted his life, as usual. She's carrying a plastic bag that has the name of a liquor store on it.

"Meetings, and the traffic was awful," she says, forty-five minutes late.

"Actually, I just got here." Win gets up, his suit covered with water spots that couldn't possibly have dried if he'd only just come in out of the rain.

She slips off her coat and it's hard not to notice what's beneath it. Lamont wears a suit better than any woman he knows. It's a shame Mother Nature wasted such good looks on her. Her name is French and she looks French, dark and exotic, sexy and seductive in a dangerous way. Had life turned out differently and Win had gone to Harvard and she wasn't so driven and selfish, they would probably get along fine and end up in bed.

She eyes his gym bag, frowns a little, says, "Now that's obsessive. You somehow fit in a workout between the airport and here?"

"Had to bring some stuff." He self-consciously shifts the bag to his other hand, careful not to clank the glass items inside it, items a tough cop like him shouldn't carry, especially not around a tough DA like Lamont.

"You can leave it in the cloakroom. Over

there by the men's room. You don't have a gun in it, do you?"

"Just an Uzi. The only thing they'll let you carry on planes anymore."

"You can hang this up while you're at it." She hands him her coat. "And this is for you."

She hands him the bag, he peeks inside, sees a bottle of Booker's bourbon in its wooden crate, expensive stuff, his favorite.

"How did you know?"

"I know a lot about my staff, make that my mission."

It rankles him to be referred to as *staff.* "Thanks," he mutters.

Inside the cloakroom, he carefully tucks the bag out of sight on top of a shelf, then follows Lamont into a dining room with candles and white cloths and waiters in white jackets. He tries not to think about his spotted suit and soaked shoes as he and Lamont sit across from each other at a corner table. It is dark out, lamps along Quincy Street blurry through the rain and fog, and people heading into the club for dinner. They don't have spots on their clothes, belong here, probably went to school here, maybe teach here, are the sort of people Monique Lamont dates or has as friends.

"At Risk," she starts in. "Our governor's new crime initiative, which he has handed off to me." She shakes open a linen napkin and drapes it over her lap as the waiter appears. "A glass of sauvignon blanc. The one from South Africa I had last time. And sparkling water."

"Iced tea," Win says. "What crime initiative?"

"Indulge yourself," she says with a smile. "We're honest tonight."

"Booker's. On the rocks," he tells the waiter.

"DNA is as old as time," she starts in. "And ancestral DNA can take the John Doe out of John Doe cases. You familiar with the new technology they're doing in some of these private labs?"

"Sure. DNAPrint Genomics in Sarasota. I've heard about a number of serial murder cases they've helped solve . . ."

She goes on without him: "Biological samples left in cases where we have no idea who the perpetrator is and come up with nothing in database searches. We retest using this cutting-edge technology.

We find out, for example, the suspect turns out to be male, eighty-two percent European, eighteen percent Native American, so we know he looks white and quite possibly we even know his hair and eye color."

"The *At Risk* part? Besides the fact the governor has to call some new initiative something, I suppose."

"It's obvious, Win. Every time we get another offender out of circulation, society is less *at risk.* The name is my idea, it's my responsibility, my project, and I intend to give it my full attention."

"With all due respect, Monique, couldn't you have just e-mailed me all this? I had to fly up here in a rainstorm all the way from Tennessee so you could tell me about the governor's latest publicity stunt?"

"I'll be brutally candid," she interrupts him, nothing new.

"You're good at brutal." He smiles at her, the waiter suddenly back with their drinks, treating Lamont like royalty.

"Let's be frank," she says. "You're reasonably intelligent. And a media dream."

It's not the first time he's thought about quitting the Massachusetts State Police. He picks up his bourbon, wishes he had ordered a double.

"There was a case in Knoxville twenty years ago. . . ." she continues.

"Knoxville?"

The waiter hovers to take their order. Win hasn't even looked at the menu.

"The bisque to start with." Lamont orders. "Salmon. Another sauvignon blanc. Give him that nice Oregon pinot."

"Whatever your steak is, rare," Win says. "A salad with balsamic vinegar. No potato. Let me see. It's just chance I happen to be sent down south to Knoxville, and suddenly you've decided to solve some cold case from down there."

"An elderly woman beaten to death," Lamont continues. "Apparently a burglary gone bad. Possible attempt at sexual assault, nude, her panties down around her knees."

"Seminal fluid?" He can't help himself. Politics or not, cases pull him in like black holes.

"I don't know the details." She reaches into her bag, pulls out a manila envelope, hands it to him.

"Why Knoxville?" He won't let it go, his paranoia clutching him harder.

"Needed was a murder and someone special to work on it. You're in Knoxville, why not see what unsolved cases they might have, and there we are. This one apparently sensational at the time, now as cold and forgotten as the victim."

"There are plenty of unsolved cases in Massachusetts." He looks at her, studies her, not sure what's really going on.

"This one should be easy."

"I wouldn't count on that."

"It works out well for a number of reasons. A failure down there won't be as obvious as one up here," she says. "The way we play it, while you were attending the Academy, you heard about the case and suggested Massachusetts could assist, try this new DNA analysis, help them out. . . ."

"So you want me to lie," he says.

"I want you to be diplomatic, smart," she says.

Win opens the envelope and slides out copies of newspaper articles, the autopsy and lab reports, none of them very good quality, probably from microfilm.

"Science," she says with confidence. "If

it's true there's a God gene, then maybe there's also a Devil gene," she adds. Lamont loves her cryptic quasi-brilliant pronouncements.

She is almost quotable.

"I'm looking for the devil that got away, looking for his ancestral DNA."

"I'm not sure why you're not using the lab in Florida that's known for all this." Win looks over the blurry copy of the autopsy report and adds, "Vivian Finlay. Sequoyah Hills. Knoxville old money on the river, can't touch a house for under a million. Someone really beat the hell out of her."

Although there are no photographs included in the records Lamont has given him, the autopsy protocol makes several things clear. Vivian Finlay survived long enough to have substantial tissue response, her face lacerated and bruised, her eyes swollen shut. When her scalp was reflected back, it revealed huge contusions, a cranium with punched-out areas caused by the repeated violent blows of a weapon that had at least one round surface.

"If we're testing for DNA, then there must be evidence. Who's had it all this time?" he asks.

"All I know is the FBI did the lab work back then."

"FBI? What interest did the Feds have?"

"I meant the state authorities," she says.

"TBI. Tennessee Bureau of Investigation."

"I don't think they were doing DNA back then."

"Nope. The dark ages when they still did good ol'fashioned serology, ABO typing. Exactly what was analyzed and who's had it all this time?" he tries again.

"Bloody clothing. As I understand it, it was still in the evidence room at the Knoxville PD, was sent to the lab in California . . ."

"California?"

"This has all been carefully researched by Huber."

Win indicates the photocopies she gave him, then asks, "This is everything?"

"Apparently the Knoxville morgue's moved since then, their old records in storage somewhere. What you've got is what Toby tracked down."

"Meaning what he had the ME's office print out from microfilm. What a sleuth," he says sarcastically. "I don't know why in the world you have an idiot like that . . ."

"You know why."

"Don't know how Huber could have an idiot son like that. You should be careful doing favors for the director of the crime labs no matter how great a guy he is, Monique. Could be construed as a conflict of interest . . ."

"How about leaving that to me," she says coldly.

"All I can say is Huber owes you big-time if he's dumped Toby on you."

"Okay. We said we're honest tonight?" She looks him in the eye, holds his gaze. "It was a bad call on my part. You're right. Toby's useless, a disaster."

"What I need is the police file. Maybe Toby the disaster got a photocopy of that, too, in the course of his arduous and thorough research?"

"I suppose you can take care of that yourself when you return to Knoxville. Toby just left for vacation."

"Poor guy. Probably exhausted from working so hard."

Lamont watches the waiter return with his silver tray and two glasses of wine, says, "You'll like the pinot. A Drouhin, the daughter, actually."

He slowly swirls it, smells it, tastes it. "Have you forgotten? You sent me to the Academy because it's the, and I quote you, *Harvard of Forensic Science.* I've got one month left."

"I'm sure they'll accommodate you, Win. Nobody said anything about your dropping out. In fact, this is going to make the NFA look good, too."

"So I'll work it in my sleep. So let's see." He sips his wine. "You're using the NFA, using the Knoxville Police Department, using me, using everyone for political gain. Tell me something, Monique." He pushes his luck, his eyes intense on hers. "Do you really give a damn about this dead old lady?"

"Headline: *BIG-SHOT MASSACHUSETTS DE-TECTIVE HELPS OUT SMALL-TOWN POLICE DE-PARTMENT, SOLVES TWENTY-YEAR-OLD CASE, VINDICATES OLD WOMAN MURDERED FOR SPARE CHANGE."*

"Spare change?"

"It's in one of the newspaper articles I gave you," she says. "Mrs. Finlay collected silver coins. Had a box of them on her dresser. The only thing missing, as far as anybody knows."

It is still raining when they leave the Harvard Faculty Club and follow old brick pavers to Quincy Street.

"Where now?" Lamont asks, half hidden by a big, black umbrella.

Win notices her tapered fingers tightly curled around the umbrella's wooden handle. Her nails are neatly squared, no polish, and she wears a large white-gold watch with a black crocodile band, a Breguet, and a Harvard signet ring. Doesn't matter what she earns as a DA and for the occasional class she teaches at the law school, Lamont comes from family money—a lot of it, from what he hears—and has a historic home near Harvard Square and the British racing green Range Rover parked across the dark, wet street.

"I'm all set," he says as if she offered him a ride. "I'll walk to the Square and grab a taxi. Or maybe stroll over to the Charles, see if they've got any good jazz going on at the Regattabar. You like Coco Montoya?"

"Not tonight."

"I didn't say he was playing tonight."

He wasn't inviting her, either.

She is digging into her coat pockets, getting impatient, looking for something, says, "Keep me informed, Win. Every detail."

"I'll go where the evidence goes. And a fine point that shouldn't get lost in all the excitement, I can't go where the evidence doesn't go."

She digs in her expensive handbag, exasperated.

"And I hate to emphasize the obvious," he says as rain falls on his bare head, trickles down his collar. "I don't see what good your At Risk initiative is going to do if we can't solve the case."

"At the very least, we'll get an ancestral DNA profile, say the case was reopened as a result. That in itself is newsworthy and compassionate, and we'll never admit to failure, just continue to keep the case open. A work in progress. You graduate from the NFA, return to your usual assignments. Eventually everybody will forget about the case all over again. . . ."

"And by then maybe you'll be governor," he says.

"Don't be so cynical. I'm not the cold-blooded person you seem determined to paint me to be. Where the hell are my keys?"

"In your hand."

"My house keys."

"Want me to go with you, make sure you get in all right?"

"I've got a spare in a key box," she says, and abruptly leaves him in the rain.

3

Win looks up and down the street, watching people moving with purpose along sidewalks, watching cars drive by, water spitting out from the tires, watching Lamont drive off.

He walks toward the Square, where the cafés and coffee shops are crowded despite the weather, and he ducks into Peet's and squeezes between people, mostly students, the privileged and self-consumed. When he orders a latte, the girl behind the counter gawks so openly at him, her face turns red. He's used to it, usually is somewhat flattered, amused, but not tonight. He can't stop thinking about Lamont and the way she makes him feel about himself.

He carries his latte through Harvard Square, where the Red Line train comes in and most people traveling on it aren't enrolled at Harvard, maybe don't even know that Harvard isn't just the local college. He loiters on the sidewalk along John F. Kennedy Street, squinting at oncoming headlights, and the rain slashing the bright lights reminds him of pencil marks, of childish drawings of falling rain, like the ones he used to draw when he was a boy, when he drew something besides crime scenes and ugly conclusions about people.

"Tremont and Broadway," he says as he climbs into a cab, carefully setting the gym bag on the vinyl bench seat.

The driver is the shape of a head talking without turning around, a Middle Eastern accent.

"Tray-mond? Where?"

"Tre-mont and Broad-way, you can drop me off on the corn-er. You don't know the way, you can stop and I'm getting out."

"Tray-mont. Is close to where?"

"In-man Square," he says loudly. "Head

that way. You can't find it, I'll walk and you don't get paid."

The driver stomps on the brake. He turns around, his dark face and dark eyes glowering at him.

"You don't pay, you get out!"

"You see this?" Win snatches out his wallet, shoves his Massachusetts State Police shield closer to the driver's face. "You want tickets the rest of your life? Your inspection sticker's expired. You realize that? One of your taillights is burned out. You aware of that? Just take me to Broadway. Think you can find the damn City Hall Annex? I'll direct you from there."

They ride in silence. Win sits in back, his hands clenched in his lap because he just had dinner with Monique Lamont, who's running for governor and oddly expects him to make Governor Crawley, who's running for reelection, look good so she'll look good, the two of them looking good when they run against each other. *Politics. Christ.* As if either one of them really cares about some murdered old lady down in the boonies of Tennessee. He gets more resentful by the moment as he sits in the dark and the taxi driver drives, having no idea where he's going unless Win tells him.

"That's Tremont there, take a right," Win finally says, pointing. "Just up there on the left. Okay, you can let me out here."

The house pains him every time he sees it, two-story, paint-peeled wood siding that is overgrown with ivy. Like the woman who lives inside, Win's family home has seen nothing but bad times for the last fifty years. He climbs out of the cab and hears the chiming of wind chimes in the dark back-yard. He sets his latte on the taxi's roof, digs in a pocket, and throws a crumpled ten-dollar bill through the driver's window.

"Hey! It's twelve dollars!"

"Hey! Get a GPS," he says as the wind chimes play their magical, airy music, as the taxi speeds off and the latte slides off the roof and pops open on the road, and milky coffee streams over the black pavement, and the chimes sweetly chime as if excited to see him.

The thick, moist air stirs and sweet, light chimes sound from the shadows and the trees, from doors and windows he can't see, chimes sound from everywhere because his grandmother believes chimes should chime all the time to ward off bad spirits, and he's never said, *Well if it really works, then how do you explain our lives?* He digs a key out of his pocket and unlocks the front door, pushes it open.

"Nana? It's me," he calls out.

Inside the foyer are the same family photographs and paintings of Jesus and crucifixes crowded over the horsehair plaster, all dusty. He shuts the door, locks it, sets his keys on an old oak table that he's looked at most of his life.

"Nana?"

The TV is on in the living room, turned up high, sirens screaming, Nana and her cop shows. The volume seems higher since he was here last, maybe because he's gotten used to quiet. Anxiety touches him as he follows the sound to the living room where nothing has changed since he was a boy except that Nana continues to accumulate crystals and stones and statues of cats and dragons and Saint Michael the Archangel and magical wreaths and bundles of herbs and incense, hundreds of all of it everywhere.

"Oh!" she exclaims when the sound of

him finally jettisons her out of some *Hill Street Blues* rerun.

"Didn't mean to startle you." He smiles, goes to the couch, and kisses her cheek.

"My darling," she says, clasping his hands.

He picks up the remote control from a table covered with more crystals and magical trinkets and stones and her deck of tarot cards. He turns off the TV and makes his usual assessment. Nana looks all right, her dark eyes alert and bright in her sharp-featured face, a face very smooth for her age, beautiful once, her long, white hair piled on top of her head. She's wearing her usual silver jewelry, bracelets practically up to her elbows, and rings and necklaces, and the blaze-orange UT football sweatshirt he sent her a few weeks ago. She never fails to put on something he gave her when she knows she'll see him. She always seems to know. He doesn't have to tell her.

"You didn't have your alarm on," he says, opening his gym bag, setting jars of sourwood honey, barbecue sauce, and bread-and-butter pickles on the coffee table.

"I have my wind chimes, darling."

It occurs to him that he left the bottle of

bourbon in the faculty club cloakroom. He didn't remember, and Lamont didn't notice that he didn't have it when they left. *That figures.*

"What did you bring me?" Nana is asking.

"I don't pay the alarm company all that money for wind chimes. Some local stuff, made right there in Tennessee. If you'd rather have moonshine, I'll bring that next time," he teases, settling in a worn-out chair she keeps covered in a purple afghan one of her clients crocheted for her a few years back.

She picks up her cards and says, "What's this about money?"

"Money?" He frowns. "Now don't go doing your juju on me, Nana."

"Something about money. You were just doing something that had to do with money."

He thinks of "Money" Monique Lamont.

"That boss lady of yours, I suppose." She slowly shuffles through her cards, her way of having a conversation, and she places a moon card next to her on the couch. "You watch out for that one. Illusions and madness or poetry and visions. You get to choose."

"How are you feeling? You eating something besides whatever people bring you?"

People give her food for readings, give her all sorts of things, whatever they can afford.

She places another card faceup on the sofa, this one a robed man carrying a lantern, and the rain has picked up again, sounds like a drumroll, tree branches scraping against window glass, wind chimes a distant, frantic clanging.

"What did she want with you?" his grandmother says. "That's who you were with tonight."

"Nothing for you to worry about. The good thing is, I get to see you."

"She keeps things hidden behind a curtain, very troublesome things, this high priestess in your life." She turns another card faceup, this one the colorful image of a man hanging by one foot from a tree, coins falling out of his pockets.

"Nana." He sighs. "She's the DA, a politician. She's not a high priestess and I don't consider her *in my life.*"

"Oh, she's in it, all right," his grandmother says, looking keenly at him. "There's someone else. I'm seeing a man in scarlet. Ha! That one goes in the freezer right away!"

His grandmother's way of taking care of destructive people is to write their names or descriptions on scraps of paper and tuck them in the freezer. Clients pay good money to have her consign their enemies to her old Frigidaire, and the last time he checked, her freezer looked like the inside of a paper-shredder basket. Win's phone vibrates and he removes it from his jacket pocket, looks at the display, the number blocked.

"Excuse me," he says, getting up, moving closer to a window, rain flailing the glass.

"Is this Winston Garano?" a man asks in a voice that is obviously disguised, a really bad fake accent that almost sounds British.

"Who wants to know?"

"I think you might want to have a coffee with me, Davis Square, the Diesel Café, where all the freaks and fags hang out. It's open late."

"Let's start with you telling me who you are."

He watches his grandmother shuffle through more tarot cards, placing them faceup on the table, thoughtful and at ease with them as if they are old friends.

"Not over the phone," the man says.

The murdered old woman suddenly enters Win's mind. He imagines her purplish-blue swollen face, the huge, dark clots on the underside of her scalp, and the holes punched into her skull, bits of bone driven into her brain. He imagines her pitiful, brutalized body on a cold steel autopsy table, doesn't know why he's suddenly thinking about her, tries to push her away.

"I don't meet strangers for coffee when they don't tell me who they are or what they want," he says into the phone.

"Vivian Finlay ring a bell? I'm pretty sure you want to talk to me."

"I'm not seeing any reason at all why I should talk to you," Win says as his grandmother sits calmly on the sofa, going through cards, placing another one faceup, this one red and white with a pentacle and a sword.

"Midnight. Be there." The man ends the call.

"Nana, I've got to go out for a while," Win says, pocketing his phone, hesitating by the rain-splattered window, getting one of his feelings, the wind chimes a discordant banging.

"Watch out for that one," she says, picking another card.

"Your car running?"

Sometimes she forgets to put gas in it, and not even divine intervention keeps the engine from quitting.

"Was last time I drove it. Who's the man in scarlet? You find that out, you tell me. You pay attention to the numbers."

"What numbers?"

"The ones coming up. Pay attention."

"Keep your doors locked, Nana," he says. "I'm setting the alarm."

Her 1989 Buick with its peeling vinyl top and rainbow bumper stickers and beaded dream catcher hanging from the rearview mirror is parked behind the house beneath the basketball hoop that's been rusting on its pole since he was a boy. The engine resists, finally gives itself up, and he backs all the way out to the street because there is no room to turn around. His headlights flash in the eyes of a dog wandering along the roadside.

"Oh for God's sake," Win says loudly as he stops the car and gets out.

"Miss Dog, what'cha doing out here, girl?" he says to the poor, wet dog. "Come here. It's me, come on, come on, that's a good girl."

Miss Dog, part beagle, part shepherd, part deaf, part blind, a name as stupid as her owner, creeps forward, sniffs Win's hand, remembers him, wags her tail. He strokes her wet, dirty fur, picks her up, and puts her in the front seat, massaging her neck as he drives her to a run-down house two blocks away. He carries her to the front door, bangs on it for a long time.

Finally, the woman inside yells, "Who is it?"

"I've got Miss Dog again!" Win yells back to her.

The door opens, the ugly, fat woman on the other side wearing a shapeless pink robe, has no bottom teeth, stinks like cigarettes. She turns on the porch light, blinks in the glare, looks past him to Nana's Buick parked on the street, never seems to remember the car or him. Win gently puts down Miss Dog and she darts inside the house, gets away from the ungrateful sloth as fast as she can.

"I told you, she's going to get hit by a car," Win warns. "What's the matter with you? This is how many times I've had to bring her home because she's wandering the damn street?"

"What am I supposed to do. I let her out to potty, she doesn't come back. Then he came over tonight, left the door open, not that he's supposed to be here. You can blame him. Kicks at her, mean as a snake, leaves the door open on purpose so she'll get out because that stupid dog gets killed it will break Suzy's heart."

"Who's he?"

"My damn son-in-law the police keep arresting."

Win thinks he might know who she's talking about, has seen him in the area, drives a white pickup.

"And you let him on the property?" Win says severely to her.

"Just try to stop him. He ain't afraid of no one, nohow. It's not me who's got the restraining order."

"You call the cops when he showed up earlier?"

"No point in it."

Through the open door, Win can see Miss Dog flat on the floor, cowering under a chair.

"How about I buy her from you," Win says.

"There's no amount of money," she retorts. "I love that dog."

"I'll give you fifty dollars."

"Can't put a price on love," she wavers.

"Sixty," he says, and that's all the cash he's got, his checkbook in Knoxville.

"No sir"—she's thinking hard about it—"my love for her's worth a whole lot more than that."

4

Two Tufts kids with green hair and tattoos clack pool balls not far from Win's table. He watches them disdainfully.

Maybe he isn't from money, didn't get sixteen hundred on his SATs or compose a symphony or build a robot, but at least when he applied to the schools of his dreams, he was respectful enough to buy a khaki suit (on sale) and new shoes (also on sale) and get a haircut (he had a five-dollar coupon) in the event he was invited by the dean of admissions to tour the campus and talk about what he wanted in life, which was to become a scholar and poet like his father, or maybe a lawyer. Win was never called for a campus tour or an interview. All he got were boilerplate letters that regretted to inform him . . .

He watches everything and everybody inside the Diesel Café, looking for a man he is supposed to meet about a murder that happened twenty years ago in Tennessee. It is almost midnight, still raining, and Win sits at his small table, sipping cappuccino, watching scruffy students with their horrible hair and grungy clothes and coffees and laptops, watching the front door, his temper heating up by the moment. At quarter past midnight, he angrily gets up from the table as some pimple-faced, thinks-he's-an-Einstein punk clumsily racks pool balls, talking loud and fast to his girlfriend, both of them oblivious, self-consumed, hyped up on something, maybe ephedrine.

"No there isn't," the girl is saying. "There's no such word as *sodomitical.*"

"*The Portrait of Dorian Gray* was called a sodomitical book." Clack. "In some of the reviews back then." A striped ball wobbles into a pocket.

"It's *Picture* of Dorian Gray, not *Portrait,* genius," Win says to the pedantic, body-pierced punk now twirling the pool cue like a baton. "And it was called a sodomitical book during Oscar Wilde's trial, not in book reviews."

"Whatever."

Win starts to walk off, catches *mulatto fag.*

He walks back, grabs the pool cue out of the punk's hands, says, "My turn to break." He snaps the pool cue in half over his knee. "Now then. You said something to me?"

"I didn't say anything!" the punk exclaims, glassy eyes huge.

Win tosses the broken halves of the pool cue on top of the table, strides off, ignores the girl behind the counter, who has been staring at him ever since he got here. She's blasting steam into a big coffee cup and says *excuse me* as he reaches for the door. *Sir?* she calls out above the noise of the espresso machine.

He walks over to the counter and says, "Don't worry. I'll pay for it." He pulls a few bills out of his wallet.

She doesn't seem interested in his pool-hall vandalism, says, "Are you Detective Geronimo?"

"Where'd you get a name like that?"

"I take that as a yes," she replies, reaching below the counter, retrieving an envelope, handing it to him. "This guy came in earlier, asked me to give this to you when you were about to leave."

"How much earlier?" He slips the envelope into a pocket, mindful of who might be watching.

"Maybe a couple hours."

So the man with the fake accent called Win *after* the letter was dropped off here, never intended on a meeting.

"What did he look like?" Win asks.

"Nothing special, kind of old. Had on tinted glasses, a big trench coat. And a scarf."

"A scarf this time of year?"

"Shiny, silky. Sort of a deep red."

"Of course." A man in scarlet, just like Nana said.

Win walks out into the rain, and the dampness of the night makes him feel sticky and wilted. His grandmother's car is a dark-finned hulk on Summer Street, in front of the Rosebud Diner, and he walks along the wet pavement, looking around, wondering if the man in scarlet is nearby, watching. He unlocks the car, opens the glove box, finds a flashlight and a stack of napkins from Dunkin' Donuts, wraps several of them around his hands, and slits open the envelope with one of the keys dangling from the steering column. He slips out a folded piece of lined paper, reads what's neatly printed on it in black ink.

You're the one AT RISK, half-breed.

He dials Lamont's home number and she doesn't answer. He tries her cell phone. She doesn't answer. He doesn't leave a message, changes his mind and tries again, and she answers this time.

"Hello?" Her voice doesn't have its usual energy.

"You want to tell me what the hell's going on!" He cranks the engine.

"No need to be upset with me," she weirdly says, sounds strained, something off about her.

"Some wacko with a wacko fake accent just called me about the Finlay case. What a coincidence. Somehow the guy has my cell-phone number, another amazing coincidence, and coincidentally said he'd meet me and didn't show up, left me a threatening note. Who the hell have you been talking to? You send out a press release or something . . . ?"

"This morning," she replies, and a muffled

male voice in the background says something Win can't make out.

"This morning? Before I even got to town!
And you couldn't bother to tell me?" he exclaims.

"That's fine," her non sequitur follows.

"It's not fine!"

The person Lamont is with—some man at
almost one o'clock in the morning—says
something and she abruptly ends the call,
and Win sits in the dark inside his grandmother's old Buick staring at the lined piece
of paper in his napkin-wrapped hands. His
heart pounds so hard he can feel it in his
neck. Lamont alerted the media about a
case that's now supposed to be his and
didn't ask his permission or even bother
telling him. She can take her At Risk shit
and shove it.

I quit.

See what she does when he tells her that.

I quit!

He has no idea where to look for her. She
didn't answer her home phone, only her cell
phone. So she probably isn't home. Well,
it's hard to say. He decides to cruise past
her Cambridge house anyway. In case she's
there. The hell with who else might be there,

and he wonders who Lamont sleeps with, if she's one of these alpha-dog women who doesn't like sex or maybe the opposite. Maybe she's a piranha, eats her lovers to the bone.

He roars away from the curb, fishtails—damn rear-wheel drive—skids on the slick pavement, and the windshield wipers drag loudly across the glass, driving him crazy because he's already feeling crazy, as if he's in the middle of something crazy that he was crazy to get in the middle of, dammit. He should have refused to fly back up here, should have stayed in Tennessee. It's late to call Sykes. It's rude. He's always doing this to her and she always lets him. She won't mind, and he enters her number, remembering it's Tuesday night, and usually on Tuesday nights at this late hour, the two of them are dressed like preppies, listening to jazz at Forty-Six-Twenty, drinking fruit-infused martinis and talking.

"Hey gorgeous," Win says. "Don't kill me."

"Figures the one time I was actually sleeping," says Sykes, an agent with the Tennessee Bureau of Investigation, and an insomniac, her hormones hateful these days.

She sits up in bed, doesn't bother with the lamp. For the past six weeks she has spent a lot of time talking to Win on the phone, in bed in the dark, alone, wondering what it would be like to talk to him in bed, in the dark, in person. She listens for her roommate through the wall, doesn't want to wake her up. The funny thing is, when Sykes drove Win to the Knoxville airport, she said to him, *Well, for once our roommates will get a full night's sleep.* Since she and Win began their training at the National Forensic Academy, they've talked the nights away, and since the student apartments don't have thick walls, their roommates get the raw end of that deal.

"I think you miss me," Sykes says, joking but hoping it's true.

"Need you to do something," Win says.

"Are you all right?" She switches on the lamp.

"I'm fine."

"You don't sound fine. What's going on?" She gets out of bed, stares at herself in the mirror over the dresser.

"Listen. An old lady was murdered in

Knoxville twenty years ago, Vivian Finlay. Sequoyah Hills."

"Let's start with why the sudden interest."

"Something damn weird's going on. You were in Tennessee back then. Maybe you remember the case."

Sykes was in Tennessee, all right, yet another reminder of her age, and she looks at herself in the mirror, her silvery blond hair sticking up everywhere, *like Amadeus* is the way Win once described it. *If you saw the movie,* he said. She hadn't.

"I vaguely recall the case," she is saying. "Rich widow, someone broke in. An unbelievable thing to happen in Sequoyah Hills in the middle of the day."

The mirror is especially unkind at this hour. Her eyes are puffy. Too much beer. She doesn't know why Win likes her so much, why he doesn't seem to see her the same way she does, maybe sees her the way she used to be, twenty years ago when she had creamy skin and big blue eyes, a tight, round butt, and perky boobs, a body that flipped the finger at gravity until she turned forty and gravity flipped the finger back.

"I need the original police file," he is saying over the phone.

"By chance you got the case number?" Sykes asks.

"Only the autopsy case number. Just microfilm print-outs from that, no scene photos, no nothing. Got to have that file too if we can ever find it in the Bermuda Triangle of storage. You know, when the old morgue moved. Or at least Lamont said it did. I'm assuming she's right."

Her again. "Yeah, it moved. Okay, one thing at a time," she says, getting stressed, irritable. "First, you want the police file."

"Got to have it, Sykes."

"So I'll try to track it down first thing in the morning."

"Can't wait. Whatever you can get your hands on now. E-mail it to me."

"And who do you think's going to help me out at this hour?" She is already opening her closet door, yanking a pair of blue cargo pants off a hanger.

"The Academy," Win says. "Call Tom, get him out of bed."

He drives fast toward Mount Auburn Hospital, turns off Brattle Street, headed to

Monique Lamont's house so he can ruin the rest of her night.

I quit.

Maybe he'll sign on with the TBI, the FBI, the FYI—*for your information, Monique, nobody jerks me around like this.*

I quit.

Then why are you sending Sykes on a mission in the middle of the night? another part of his brain asks him. A minor technicality. Just because he quits Lamont doesn't mean he'll quit the Vivian Finlay case. It's personal now. Some man in scarlet screws with him, insults him, and it gets personal. Win drives through an intersection, barely slows at the stop sign, turns left near the fire station, onto the narrow street where Lamont lives on a sliver of an acre in a nineteenth-century pale plum house, a Queen Anne Painted Lady, showy and intricate and formidable, like its owner. Her property is dense with crepe myrtles, oaks and birch trees, and the dark shapes of them rock in the wind and water drips from branches and leaves.

He parks in front, turns off his headlights, cuts the engine. The front porch light isn't on, no lights along the property are on, and only one window is lit up, the one on the second floor to the left of the front door, and he has one of his feelings. Her Range Rover is in the cobbled driveway, and his feeling intensifies. If she's not home, somebody picked her up. Well, big deal. She could have anybody she wants, so her date du jour picked her up, maybe took her to his place, big deal, but the feeling persists. If her date du jour is inside the house with her, where's his car? Win tries her home phone and gets voicemail. He tries her cell phone and she doesn't answer. He tries it a second time. She doesn't answer.

Some man in a red scarf sending him on a wild-goose chase, making a fool of him, threatening him, taunting him. *Who?* Win worries about what's going to appear in the news. Maybe Lamont's idiotic press release is screaming through cyberspace, landing all over the Internet. Maybe that's how the man in the red scarf found out about At Risk, about Win, but it doesn't make sense. As far as he knows, Vivian Finlay wasn't from New England, so why is some man in New England interested enough in her case to go to all the trouble to call Win, set up a phony meeting, and taunt him?

He continues staring at Lamont's house, at her densely wooded property, looking up and down the street—for what, he doesn't know. For anything. He grabs the flashlight and gets out of his grandmother's prehistoric-looking car, keeping up his scan, listening. Something doesn't feel right, feels worse than not right. Maybe he's just rattled, expecting something not to feel right, getting spooked the way he did as a boy when he started imagining monsters, bad people, bad things, death, having premonitions because *it's in his blood,* as his grandmother so often declared. He has no gun. He follows the brick walk to the front porch, climbs the steps, looking, listening, deciding that what he's really uneasy about is Lamont.

She won't be nice about this. If she's with someone, she'll have Win's head. He starts to ring the bell, looks up at the same time a shadow moves past the curtained, lighted window directly overhead. He stares up, waiting. He shines the flashlight at the brass mailbox to the left of the front door, lifts the lid. She didn't pick up her mail when she came in, and he remembers what she said about a key box. He doesn't see anything like that.

Water drips in big, cool drops from leaves and smacks the top of his head as he goes around to the back of the house, where it is thickly wooded and very dark, where he finds the key box open, the key still in the lock, the door ajar. He hesitates, looks around, listening to water dripping, shining the flashlight in the trees, the shrubbery, directing the beam back to something dark red between two boxwoods, a gas can with rags on top of it, wet from the rain but clean. His pulse picks up, begins to race as he silently steps into the kitchen, hears Lamont's voice, then a male voice, an angry male voice, on the second floor, the room with the lighted window above the front door.

He moves fast up wooden stairs that creak, three stairs at a time, cuts across a hallway that creaks. Through an open doorway he sees her on the bed, nude, tied to the bedposts, a man in jeans, a T-shirt, sitting on the edge of the bed, stroking her with a pistol.

"Say it, *I'm a whore.*"

"I'm a whore," she repeats in a shaky voice. "Please don't do this."

Left of the bed is the window, the drapes

drawn. Her clothes are strewn on the floor, the same suit she had on hours earlier at dinner.

"I'm nothing but a filthy whore. Say it!"

Overhead is a large art glass chandelier with painted flowers—blue, red, green—and Win hurls the flashlight and it crashes into the chandelier and it shatters and sways and the man jumps up from the bed, whips around, and then Win has him by the wrist, struggling to get the pistol away from him, the man's breath in his face, reeking of garlic, and the gun fires into the ceiling, just missing Win's head.

"Drop it! Drop it!"

His voice sounds muffled and distant in his ringing ears as he struggles, and the pistol fires again and again and the man's grip suddenly goes limp. Win grabs hold of the gun, shoves him hard and he collapses to the floor, blood flowing out of his head, pooling on the hardwood, quiet on the floor next to the bed, bleeding, not moving, a young, Hispanic-looking man, maybe in his teens.

Win yanks a comforter over Lamont, frees her from the electrical cords lashing her to the bedposts as he repeatedly says, "It's all right. You're safe now. It's all right." He calls 911 on his cell phone and she sits up, pulling the comforter around her, gasping for breath, shaking violently, eyes wild.

"Oh God," she says. "Oh God!" she screams.

"It's okay, it's okay, you're safe now," he says, standing over her, looking around, watching the man on the floor, blood and bloody shards of colorful art glass everywhere.

"Is he the only one?" Win yells at Lamont as his heart pounds and his eyes dart around, his ears ringing, the pistol ready. "Is there anybody else?" he shouts.

She shakes her head, her breathing rapid and shallow, her face blanched, her eyes glazed, about to pass out.

"Deep, slow breaths, Monique." Win takes off his suit jacket, places it in her hands, helps her hold it up to her face. "It's all right. Breathe into it like it's a paper bag. That's good. Good. Deep, slow breaths. No one's going to hurt you now."

5

Monique Lamont wears a hospital gown inside an examination room at Mount Auburn
Hospital, but a few blocks from where she
lives.

It is a nondescript room, white, with an
examination table, the kind with stirrups,
and a counter, a sink, a cabinet filled with
medical supplies, swabs and specula, a
surgical lamp. Moments earlier, a forensic
nurse was alone in the room with Lamont,
examining the powerful district attorney's
orifices and other very private areas of her
body, swabbing for saliva and seminal fluid,
plucking hairs, getting fingernail scrapings,

looking for injuries, taking photographs, gathering whatever might be potential evidence. Lamont is holding up amazingly well, maybe bizarrely well, playing the role of herself, working her own case.

She sits in a white plastic chair next to the white paper-covered table, Win on a stool across from her, another investigator with the Massachusetts State Police, Sammy, standing near the shut door. She had the option of being interviewed in more civilized surroundings, her home, for example, but refused, made the rather chillingly clinical observation that it was best to compartmentalize, keep related conversations and activities to the confined spaces where they belong. Translated: Win seriously doubts she'll ever sleep in her bedroom again. He won't be surprised if she sells her house.

"What do we know about him?" she asks again, the prosecutor who seems to have no feelings about what just happened.

Her attacker is in critical condition. Win is careful what he tells her. It is, to say the least, a highly unusual situation. She is accustomed to asking the state police anything she wants and having nothing withheld from her. She is the district attorney, is in charge, is programmed to demand details and get them.

"Ms. Lamont," Sammy says respectfully, "as you know, he had a gun and Win here did what he had to do. Things happen."

But that's not what she's asking. She looks at Win, holds his gaze remarkably well considering that just hours ago he saw her nude, lashed to her bed.

"What do you know about him." She poses it not as a question but a command.

"This much," Win says. "Your office prosecuted him in juvenile court about two months ago."

"For what?"

"Possession of marijuana, crack. Judge Let-'em-Loose Lane gave him a reprimand."

"The prosecutor certainly wasn't me. I've never seen him before. What else?"

"Tell you what," Win says. "How about letting us get our job done first, then I'll tell you anything I can."

"No," she says. "It won't be what you can. It will be what I ask."

"But for now . . ." Win starts to say.

"Information," she demands.

"I got a question." It is Sammy who says

this from his remote position near the wall. "About your getting home last night."

His ruddy face is grim, something in his eyes. Maybe it's embarrassment. Maybe talking to the district attorney after she's been through something like this somehow makes him a voyeur. Lamont ignores him, ignores his question.

"I had dinner with you," she says to Win. "I got in my car and drove back to the office to finish up a few things, then drove straight home. Because I didn't have my keys, I went around to the back of the house, put my code into the key box, got out the spare key, and was unlocking the back door when suddenly a hand clamped over my mouth and someone I couldn't see said *one sound, you're dead.* He pushed me into the house."

Lamont does a fine job reciting the facts. Her assailant, now identified as Roger Baptista of East Cambridge, an address not far from the court building where Lamont works, forced her up to her bedroom, began yanking electrical cords from lamps, from the clock radio. Then her home phone rang. She didn't answer it. Then her cell phone rang. She didn't answer it.

Win calling her.

Her cell phone rang again and she thought fast, said it was her boyfriend, he was getting worried, might show up, so Baptista told her to answer the phone and if she tried anything he'd blow her head off and then kill her boyfriend, kill everybody, and she answered. She had the brief, peculiar conversation with Win. She says she ended the call and Baptista forced her to undress and tied her to the bedposts. He raped her. Then put his pants back on.

"Why didn't you resist?" Sammy asks her as delicately as possible.

"He had a gun." She looks at Win. "I had no doubt he would use it if I resisted, probably would use it, regardless. When he finished with me. I did what I could to control the situation."

"Meaning?" Win asks.

She hesitates, her eyes cutting away from him, says, "Meaning, I told him to do what he wanted, acted as if I wasn't frightened. Or repulsed. Did what he wanted. Said what he told me to say." She hesitates. "As calm and noncombative as I could muster under the circumstances. I, uh, I said it wasn't necessary to tie me up, I, well, I worked with cases like this all the time, understood them, knew he had his reasons. I, well, I . . ."

The small room echoes with the ensuing silence and it is the first time Win has ever seen Lamont's face turn red. He suspects he knows exactly what she did to stall Baptista, to calm him, to connect with him in the remote hope he would let her live.

"Maybe you acted like you wanted a little," Sammy suggests. "Hey, women do it all the time, make the rapist think it's okay, they're good in bed, fake an orgasm and even ask the guy to come back another time like it's a date or . . ."

"Out!" Lamont fires at him, pointing her finger. "Get out!"

"I'm just—"

"Didn't you hear me?"

He leaves the room, leaves Win alone with her, not his first choice. Considering he critically injured her assailant, it would be preferable and prudent to interview her with at least one witness present.

"Who is this piece of shit?" Lamont asks. "Who? And do you think it's a goddamn coincidence he decided to show up at the house the same night my keys mysteriously disappeared? Who is he?"

"Roger Baptista . . ."

"That's not what I'm asking."

"When's the last time you saw your keys?" Win says. "You lock up with them when you left for work this morning? Actually, yesterday morning."

"No."

"No?"

She is silent for a moment, then, "I didn't come home that night."

"Where were you?"

"I stayed with a friend. Left there for work in the morning. After work I had dinner with you, checked by my office. That's the chronology."

"You mind telling me who you stayed with?"

"I do."

"I'm just trying . . ."

"I'm not the one who committed a crime." She stares coldly at him.

"Monique, I assume your alarm was set when you unlocked the door with your spare key," Win pointedly says. "Baptista clamps his hand over your mouth as you're unlocking the door. So what about the alarm after that?"

"He told me if I didn't disarm it he'd kill me."

"No panic code that silently alerts the police?"

"Oh for God's sake. And you would think of that if it were you? See what security precautions you revert to when someone's got a gun to the back of your head."

"You know anything about a can of gasoline and some rags found by your back door, in the bushes?"

"You and I need to have a very important conversation," she says to him.

Sykes drives her personal car, a '79 blue VW Rabbit, through the Old City, as Knoxville's historic downtown is called.

She passes Barley's Taproom & Pizzeria, the Tonic Grill, deserted and dark, then a construction site that was shut down the other day when a backhoe dug up bones that turned out to be cow, the site having been a slaughterhouse and stockyard in a long-ago life. Her uneasiness—the jitters, as she calls them—gets worse the closer she gets to where she's going. She sure hopes Win's insistence that she track down the

Vivian Finlay case records *immediately* is really urgent enough to merit her waking up the Academy director, then the chief of the Knoxville Police Department, next several other people with the Criminal Investigative Division and Records, who couldn't find the case, only its accession number, KPD893-85.

Last and most unpleasant of all, Sykes woke up former detective Jimmy Barber's widow, who sounded drunk, and asked what her late husband might have done with his old files, paperwork, memorabilia, et cetera, when he retired and packed up his office at headquarters.

All that crap's in the basement. What you people think he's hiding down there, Jimmy Hoffla? The damn Da Vinshay code?

I sure am sorry to bother you, ma'am. But we're trying to locate some old records, careful what she said, mindful that Win made it clear something unusual is going on.

I don't know what's got such a bug up y'all's butt, Mrs. Barber complained over the phone, swearing, slurring, nasty. *It's three damn o'clock in the morning!*

In what the locals call Shortwest Knoxville,

the city begins to fray around the edges, disintegrating into housing projects before it improves a little, not much, about two miles west of downtown. Sykes parks in front of a small rancher, vinyl siding, the yard a mess, the only house with empty supercans haphazardly parked near the street because Mrs. Barber is too lazy to roll them back to the house, it seems. The neighborhood has very few streetlights and a lot of souped-up gaudy old cars—Cadillacs, a Lincoln painted purple, a Corvette with those stupid spinning hubcaps. The crapmobiles of dirtbags, drug dealers, no-account kids. Sykes is mindful of the Glock .40-caliber pistol in the shoulder holster under her jacket. She follows the sidewalk and rings the bell.

Momentarily, the porch light blinks on.

"Who is it?" a voice slurs from the other side of the door.

"Agent Sykes, Tennessee Bureau of Investigation."

A burglar chain rattles. A dead-bolt lock snaps free. The door opens and a cheap-looking woman with dyed blond hair and makeup smudges under her eyes steps aside to let Sykes in.

"Mrs. Barber," Sykes politely says. "I sure appreciate . . ."

"I don't get what all the fuss is about, but go on." Her housecoat is buttoned crooked, eyes bloodshot, smells like booze. "The basement's thataway," she indicates with a nod, fumbles to relock the door, has a very loud voice with a very strong twang. "Rummage through his junk all you want. You can load it in a truck and haul it the hell away for all I care."

"I won't be needing to load it in a truck," Sykes says. "I just need to look through some police files he may have had in his office once."

"I'm going back to bed," Mrs. Barber says.

Lamont seems to have forgotten where she is.

It crosses Win's mind that she's delusional, believes she's in her big office surrounded by her big glass collection, maybe in one of her big-ticket designer suits, sitting at her big glass desk instead of in a hospital gown, in a plastic chair, inside a hospital examination room. She acts as if she and Win are doing their usual thing, working a high-profile case, a bad one destined for a lot of complications and press.

"I'm not sure you're hearing me," she says to Win as a knock sounds on the shut door.

"Just a minute." He gets up to answer it.

It's Sammy, pokes his head in, quietly says, "Sorry."

Win steps out into the corridor, pulls the door shut. Sammy hands him this morning's *Boston Globe,* the local section. The headline across the top of the front page is big and bold.

ANY CRIME, ANY TIME
DA ENLISTS SPACE-AGE SCIENCE
TO SOLVE OLD MURDER

"Four things you should know," Sammy says. "First, your name's all over this thing, a damn road map for how you're supposedly going to solve the governor's whodunit. More accurate, *her* whodunit"—he looks at the shut door—"since he's delegated it to her. Good luck if the killer's still out there and reads all this shit. Second, well, the second thing's sure as hell not good."

"What?"

"Baptista just died. To state the obvious, now we don't get to talk to him. Third, I went through his clothes, found a thousand bucks in hundred-dollar bills in his back pocket."

"Loose, folded up, what?"

"Plain white envelope, no writing on it. Bills new-looking, you know, crisp. Not folded or nothing. I called Huber at home. The labs are going to process them right away, look for prints."

"What's the fourth thing?"

"The media's found out about . . ." He again nods toward the shut door. "There's like three TV trucks and a crowd of reporters out there in the parking lot and it isn't even daylight yet."

Win steps back inside the examination room, shuts the door.

Lamont is sitting in the same plastic chair. It occurs to him she's got nothing to wear unless she can handle the warm-up suit she put on before he drove her to the hospital. After the assault, she couldn't shower, he didn't have to give her instructions, she knows the routine. She still hasn't showered, and it's not a subject he is entirely comfortable bringing up.

"The press has found out," he says, sitting back down on the stool. "I need to get you out of here without them ambushing you. I'm sure you know you can't go back to your house right now."

"He was going to burn it down," she states.

The gas can was full. It certainly wasn't left there by her yardman.

"He was going to kill me and burn down my house." A steady, firm voice, the DA working the case as if she's talking about some other victim. "Why? To make my death look like an accident. To make it look like I burned up in my house. He's no beginner."

"Depends on whether it was his idea," Win says. "Or if someone gave him instructions. In any event, disguising a homicide with fire isn't very reliable. Most likely, the autopsy would have revealed soft-tissue injury, the bullet, and possible damage to cartilage, bone. Bodies don't completely burn up in house fires. You know that."

He thinks about the money in Baptista's pocket, something telling him it's not a good idea to give that detail to Lamont just yet.

"I need you to stay here," she says, tightly gripping the blanket she holds around herself. "Forget the lady in Tennessee, what's-her-name. We need to find out who's behind this. Not just some little nobody piece of . . . maybe someone else who put him up to it."

"Huber's already getting the labs mobilized . . ."

"How does he know about it?" she blurts out. "I haven't told—" She stops short, her eyes wide. "He's not going to get away with this," and she's talking about Baptista again. "This is one case that isn't going to be . . . I want you in charge of it. We're going to bury him."

He resists the obvious pun, says, "Monique, he's dead."

She doesn't flinch.

"Justified or not, struggle or not, I killed him. It was a good shooting. But you know what happens. Your office can't investigate it alone, will either have to transfer the case to another DA's office or bring in the Boston Homicide Unit. Not to mention Internal Affairs doing its thing. Not to mention the autopsy and every other test known to man. I'll be put on administrative duties for a while."

"I want you on this right now."

"Not even a mental-health day? That's nice."

"Go drink a few beers with the stress unit. I don't want to hear about your so-called mental health." Her face is livid now, her eyes dark holes of hate, as if he is the one who attacked her. "If I don't get a mental-health day, I'll be damned if you do."

Her change in demeanor is startling, unnerving.

"Maybe you don't grasp the magnitude of what just happened," he says. "I see it all the time with other victims."

"I'm not a victim. I was victimized." Just as suddenly, she is the DA again, the strategist, the politician. "This has to be handled precisely right or you know what I'll be known for? The gubernatorial candidate who was raped."

He doesn't reply

"Any crime, any time, including mine," she says.

6

Monique stands in the middle of the examination room, the white blanket wrapped around her.

"Get us out of here," she says to Win.

"It's not *us*," he says. "I can't be involved. . . ."

"I want you in charge of this. Now come with me," she says, her face calm, masklike. "Get us out of here. Stay with me until I know I'm safe. We don't know who's behind this. I must be safe."

"You'll be safe, but I can't be your protection."

She stares at him.

"I've got to let them investigate this, Monique. I can't be involved in a deadly-force case and go about my business as if nothing happened."

"You can and you will."

"You're not really expecting me to be your bodyguard . . . ?"

"That would be your fantasy, wouldn't it," she says, and she stares at him, something in her eyes he's never seen before, not from her. "Get me out of here. There must be a basement, a fire exit, something, get me out of here. Doesn't this goddamn hospital have a rooftop helipad?"

Win calls Sammy on the cell phone, says, "Get one of the choppers in and fly her out of here."

"To where?" Sammy asks.

Win looks at Lamont, says, "You got some safe place to stay?"

She hesitates, then, "Boston."

"Where in Boston? I need to know."

"An apartment."

"You have an apartment in Boston?" That's news to him. Why would she have an apartment less than ten miles from her house?

She doesn't reply, doesn't owe him any further explanations about her life.

He tells Sammy, "Get an officer to meet her when she lands, escort her to her apartment."

He gets off the phone, looks at her, has one of his bad feelings, says, "Words aren't enough, Monique, but I can't tell you how sorry . . ."

"You're right, words aren't enough." She gives him the same disconcerting stare.

"I'm out of commission for a few days, starting now," he says. "It's the best thing to do."

Her eyes bore into him as she stands in the small, white room, the white blanket wrapped around her.

"What do you mean, *the best thing*? I should think I'm the one who decides what the best thing is for me."

"Maybe this isn't only about you," he says.

Her scary eyes don't leave his.

"Monique, I need a few days to take care of things."

"Right now, your job is to take care of me," she says. "We have to do damage control, turn this into something positive. *You* need *me.*"

She stands perfectly still, her eyes staring. Behind them is a darkness seething with hatred and rage.

"I'm the only witness," she states in a flat tone.

"Are you threatening to lie about what happened if I don't do what you say?"

"I don't lie. That's one thing people know about me," she replies.

"You're threatening me?" He says it again, and now he's a cop, now he isn't the man who saved her life. "Because there are more important witnesses than you. The silent witnesses of forensic science. His body fluids, for example. Unless you're going to say it was consensual. Then I guess his saliva, his seminal fluid are irrelevant. Then I guess I inadvertently interrupted a tryst, some creative sex scenario. Maybe he thought he was protecting you from me, thought I was the intruder, instead of the other way around. That what you're going to say, Monique?"

"How dare you."

"I'm pretty good with scripts. You want a few more?"

"How dare you!"

"No. How dare you. I just saved your god-damn life."

"You sexist pig. Typical man. Think all of us want it."

"Stop it."

"Think all of us have some secret fantasy about being . . ."

"Stop it!" Then he lowers his voice. "I'll help you all I can. I didn't do this to you. You know what happened. He's dead. He got what he deserved. The best revenge, if you want to look at it that way. You won, made him pay the ultimate price, if you want to look at it that way. Now let's repair what we can, get things on the right track as best we can. Damage control, as you put it."

Her eyes clear. Thoughts move in them.

"I need a few days," Win says. "I need you to refrain from taking this out on me. If you can't do that, I'll have no choice but to . . ."

"Facts," she interrupts him. "Fingerprints on the gas can. DNA. The pistol—is it stolen? My missing keys, probably a coincidence unless they were on his person, in his residence. If so, why wasn't he waiting inside my house?"

"Your alarm."

"Right." She paces, wrapped in her white blanket like an Indian chief. "How did he get to my house. Does he have a car. Did someone else drive him. His family. Who did he know."

Past tense. Her attacker is dead and she thinks of him as dead already. It hasn't even been an hour. Win looks at his watch. He calls Sammy. The chopper's nine minutes out.

The Bell 430 lifts off from Mount Auburn Hospital's rooftop helipad, hovers and noses around, flies off toward the Boston skyline. It's a seven-million-dollar bird. Lamont had a lot to do with making sure the Massachusetts State Police has three of them.

At the moment she doesn't take much pride in that, doesn't take much pride in anything, isn't sure how she feels except heavy, stony. From where she sits in back, she can see frantic journalists on the ground, their cameras pointed in her loud, dramatic direction, and she shuts her eyes and tries to ignore her desperate need for a shower and clean clothing, tries to ignore areas of her body that were invaded and violated, tries to ignore nagging fears about sexually transmitted diseases, pregnancy. She tries to concentrate on who and what she is and not on what happened hours earlier.

She takes a deep breath, looks out the window, looks at the rooftops passing below her as the helicopter beats its way toward Massachusetts General Hospital, where the pilots plan to land so some state policeperson can pick her up and transport her to an apartment no one is supposed to know about. She'll probably pay for that mistake, doesn't know what else she could have done.

"You all right back there?" A pilot's voice sounds through her headset.

"Fine."

"We'll be landing in four minutes."

She is sinking. She stares without blinking at the partition that separates the pilots from her, and she feels herself getting heavier, sinking lower. Once when she was an undergraduate at Harvard she got drunk, really drunk, and although she never said a word about it to anyone, she knew that at least one of the men she was partying with had sex with her while she was unconscious. When she came to, the sun was up and the birds were making noise, and she was alone on a couch and it was obvious what had happened, but she didn't accuse the suspect she had in mind, certainly didn't consider an examination by a forensic nurse. She remembers how she felt that day—poisoned, dazed. No, not just dazed, maybe dead. That was it, she recalls as she flies into the downtown skyline. She felt dead.

Death can be liberating. There are things you don't have to care about anymore if you're dead. People can't injure or maim parts of you that are dead.

"Ms. Lamont?" A pilot's voice sounds in her headset again. "When we land, it will take us a minute to shut down and I want you to sit tight. Someone will open the door for you and get you out."

She imagines Governor Crawley. She imagines his ugly, smirking face when he hears the news. He probably already knows. Of course he does. He'll be sympathetic, heartbroken, and degrade and destroy her in the election.

"Then what?" she says, pushing the mic close to her lip.

"The state police officer on the ground will tell you. . . ." one of the pilots answers.

"You're the state police," she says. "I'm asking you what the plan is. Is the media there?"

"You'll be briefed, I'm sure, ma'am."

They are hovering over the hospital's rooftop helipad now, a blaze-orange windsock whipping around in the rotor wash, some state policewoman in a blue uniform bending her head against the wind. The helicopter sets down, goes into flight idle, and Lamont sits, staring out at the unfamiliar, plain-looking woman officer, someone low on the food chain who's supposed to get the traumatized and besieged DA to safe asylum. A damn escort, a damn bodyguard, a damn woman to remind Lamont that she's a woman who has just been violated by a man and therefore most likely doesn't want to be escorted by a man. She's damaged. A victim. She imagines Crawley, imagines what he'll say, what he's already saying and thinking.

The engines go silent, the blades whining quietly, winding down, then braking to a stop. She takes off her headset and shoulder harness and imagines Crawley's smarmy, pious face looking into the camera and offering compassion from the people of Massachusetts to Monique Lamont. Victim Lamont.

Victim Lamont for governor. Any crime, any time, including mine.

Lamont opens the helicopter door herself before the officer can, climbs out herself before anybody can help her.

Any crime, any time, including mine Lamont.

"I want you to find Win Garano for me. Right now," Lamont says to the officer. "Tell him to drop everything he's doing and call me right now," she orders.

"Yes, ma'am. I'm Sergeant Small." The woman in blue offers a handshake, does everything but salute.

"An unfortunate name," Lamont says, walking off toward a door that leads inside the hospital.

"You mean the investigator, right? The one they call Geronimo." Sergeant Small catches up with her. "If I was fat it would be a really unfortunate name, ma'am. I get made fun of enough." She removes her radio from her big black belt, opening the door. "I've got my car downstairs, hid out of view. You mind some stairs? Then where can I take you?"

"The *Globe*," she says.

Jimmy Barber's basement is dusty and mildewy with nothing but one low-wattage bare bulb to illuminate what must be a hundred cardboard cartons stacked to the rafters, some labeled, most not.

Sykes has spent the past four hours pushing aside boxes of miscellaneous crap—ancient tape recorders, scores of tapes, several empty flowerpots, fishing tackle, baseball caps, an old-style bulletproof vest, softball trophies, what must be thousands of photographs and letters and magazines, files, notepads, the handwriting horrible. Crap and more crap. The man was too lazy to organize his memorabilia so he just threw it into boxes, packed up everything short of fast-food wrappers and what was in his wastepaper basket.

So far, she's been through plenty of cases, ones he probably thought were worth saving: a fugitive who hid in a chimney and got stuck, a deadly assault with a bowling pin, a man struck by lightning while sleeping in an iron bed, an intoxicated woman who stopped in the middle of a road to pee, forgot to put her car in gear, ran over herself. Cases and more cases that Barber shouldn't have decided were his to carry home when he retired. But she has yet to find KPD893-85, not even in a box that contained a lot of papers, correspondence, and cases for 1985. She calls Win's cell phone for the third time, leaves another message, knows he's busy but takes it personally.

She can't help thinking that if she were someone really important, maybe like that Harvard-educated woman DA he complains about so much, he'd call back promptly. Sykes went to a tiny Christian college in Bristol, Tennessee, flunked out her second year, hated school, didn't see a practical reason in the world why she should learn French or calculus or go to chapel twice a week. She's not the same caliber as Win and that DA and all those other people way up north who are part of his life. She's practically old enough to be his mother.

Sykes sits on top of an overturned five-gallon plastic pickle bucket, staring at stacks of cardboard boxes, her throat scratchy, her eyes itchy, her lower back aching. For a moment she is overwhelmed, not merely by the task before her but by everything, sort of the way she felt when she began the Academy and on day two, the class was taken on a tour of that notorious University of Tennessee research facility known as The Body Farm, two wooded acres littered with stinking dead bodies in every condition imaginable, donated human remains rotting on the ground or under concrete slabs or in car trunks or in bodybags or out of bodybags, clothed or naked, anthropologists and entomologists wandering around day after day, taking notes.

Who could do this? I mean, what kind of person does something this disgusting for a living or graduate school or whatever? she asked Win as they crouched down, looking at maggots teeming over a partially skeletonized man whose hair had slid off his skull, looked like roadkill, about three feet away.

Better get used to it, he said as if the stench, the insects didn't bother him at all, said it as if she didn't know squat. *Dead people aren't nice to work with and they never say thanks. Maggots are good. Just little babies. See?* He picked one up, put it on his fingertip, where it perched like a grain of rice, a wiggly one. *Snitches. Our little friends. Tell us time of death, all kinds of things.*

I can hate maggots all I want, Sykes said. *And I don't need you treating me like I just fell off the turnip truck.*

She gets up from her pickle bucket, surveys layers of boxes, wondering which ones contain more old cases that walked out of the office with Detective Barber. Selfish, pinheaded idiot. She lifts a box four layers up, grunting under the weight of it, hoping she doesn't pull something. Most of the boxes are open, probably because the old goat couldn't bother re-taping them shut after going in and out of them over the years, and she starts rummaging through charge-card statements and phone and utility bills going back to the mid-eighties. It's not what she's looking for, but the funny thing about bills and receipts is that they often reveal more about a person than confessions and eyewitness accounts, and she entertains an idle curiosity as she imagines August 8 twenty years ago, the day Vivian Finlay was murdered.

She imagines Detective Barber going to

work that day, probably as if it were any other day, and then getting called to Mrs. Finlay's expensive riverfront home in Sequoyah Hills. Sykes tries to remember where she was twenty years ago in August. Getting divorced, that's where. Twenty years ago she was a police dispatcher in Nashville and her husband worked for a recording company, exposing himself to new female talent in a way that turned out to be a little different from what Sykes thought was acceptable.

She pulls out files sloppily labeled by month and sits back down on the pickle bucket with credit-card receipts and utility and telephone bills. The address on the envelopes is the one for the house that belongs to this hellhole of a basement, and as she looks over MasterCard charges, she begins to suspect that Barber lived alone back then, most of his charges made at places like Home Depot, Wal-Mart, a liquor store, a sports bar. She notes that throughout the first half of 1985, he made very few long-distance calls, in some months no more than two or three. Then in August, that abruptly changed.

She shines the flashlight on a phone bill and recalls that twenty years ago cell phones were these big, cumbersome contraptions that looked like a Geiger counter. Nobody used them. Cops didn't. When they were away from their desks and needed to make calls they asked the dispatcher to do it and relay the information over the radio. If the information the detective needed was confidential or involved, he returned to headquarters, and if he was on the road, he charged the calls to the department and then had to fill out forms for reimbursement.

What cops didn't do was make case-related calls from their homes or charge them to their home numbers, but beginning the evening of August 8, when Mrs. Finlay was already dead and in the morgue refrigerator, Barber started making calls from his home phone, seven of them between five p.m. and midnight.

7

Win's condo is on the third floor of a brick-and-sandstone building that in the mid-eighteen-hundreds was a school. For someone who had so much trouble getting into schools, it's strange that he ended up living in one.

It wasn't premeditated. When he was hired by the Massachusetts State Police, he was twenty-two, had nothing to his name but a ten-year-old Jeep, secondhand clothes, and the five hundred dollars that Nana had scraped together for a college graduation present. Finding an affordable place in Cambridge was out of the question until he happened upon the old schoolhouse on Orchard Street, abandoned for decades, then being converted into condominiums. The building wasn't habitable yet, and Win made a deal with Farouk, the owner: If the rent was sufficiently cheap and Farouk promised not to raise it more than three percent per year, Win would live there during the extensive renovation and provide security and supervision.

Now his police presence is enough. He doesn't have to supervise anything and Farouk lets him park his Hummer H2 (seized from a drug dealer and sold at auction for a song), his Harley-Davidson Road King (repossessed, gently used), and his unmarked police car in a small paved area in back. None of the other tenants have parking, fight it out along the narrow street, get dinged and crunched and scraped.

Win unlocks the back door and walks up three flights of stairs to a hallway lined with units that once were classrooms. He lives at the end of the hall, number 31. He unlocks the heavy oak door and steps inside a private enclave of old brick walls that still have the original chalkboards built into them, and fir floors and wainscoting and vaulted ceilings. His furniture isn't of the period, a brown leather Ralph Lauren couch (second-hand), a chair and Oriental rug (eBay), a Thomas Moser coffee table (floor sample, slightly damaged). He looks, listens, engages all of his senses. The air seems stagnant, the living room lonely, and he retrieves a flashlight from a drawer, shines it obliquely over the floor, the furniture, the windows, looking for footprints or fingermarks in dust or on shiny surfaces. He doesn't have an alarm system, can afford just the one in Nana's house. Doesn't matter, he has his own way of dealing with intruders.

Inside the coat closet near the front door, he opens a safe built into the wall, gets out his Smith & Wesson .357, model 340, internal hammer, or "hammerless," so it doesn't get snagged on clothing, and constructed of a titanium and aluminum alloy, so lightweight it feels like a toy. He tucks the revolver into a pocket and walks into the kitchen, fixes a pot of coffee, looks through mail Farouk has stacked on the counter, most of it magazines, thumbs through *Forbes* while coffee drips, skims an article on the fastest cars, Porsche's new 911, the new Mercedes SLK55, Maserati Spyder.

He heads into his bedroom with its brick

walls, another chalkboard (for keeping score, he tells some of the women he dates, winks at them, just kidding), sits on the bed, sips coffee, thinking, his eyes heavy.

Sykes wishes she had thought of bringing a bottle of water with her and something to eat. Her mouth is dry, tastes like dust. Her blood sugar's dropping.

Several times she has thought about venturing upstairs again and asking Detective Jimmy Barber's widow for a little hospitality, but the one time she went up to inquire if she could use the bathroom, Mrs. Barber, who was supposed to be asleep, was sitting at the kitchen table, drinking straight vodka and as unfriendly and unpleasant as a skunk.

"Go on." Drunk as hell, jerks her head toward the bathroom down the hall. "Then get on with your business and leave me the hell alone. I'm sick and tired of all this, done my bit."

Alone and exhausted in the basement, Sykes continues studying Barber's baffling phone bills, trying to make sense of his charging so many of them to his home phone. Five of them have the area code 919, the same number each time, and Sykes tries it, gets an answering service for the North Carolina State Medical Examiner's Office, someone asking if she wants to report a case.

"No. Oh, I'm sorry," she says. "I must have the wrong number," and she hangs up.

She notes that at least a dozen other calls Barber charged to his home phone over the days after Vivian Finlay's murder have the area code 704. She tries the number and gets a recording—the area code has been changed to 828. She redials.

"Hello?" a groggy male voice answers.

Sykes checks her watch. It's almost seven a.m., says, "Really sorry to bother you so early, sir. But do you mind telling me how long you've had this phone number?"

He hangs up on her. Maybe it wasn't the best approach. She tries again and says right off, "I promise this isn't a crank call, sir. I'm an agent with the Tennessee Bureau of Investigation and I've come across this phone number in a case I'm looking at."

"Good Lord," he says. "You're kidding."

"No sir. Serious as a heart attack. A case that happened twenty years ago."

"Good Lord," he says. "You must mean my aunt."

"And that would be . . . ?" Sykes asks.

"Vivian Finlay. This number was hers. I mean, we've never changed it."

"So I'm assuming she had another home besides the one in Knoxville."

"That's right. Here in Flat Rock. I'm her nephew."

Sykes calmly asks, "Do you remember Jimmy Barber, the detective who worked your aunt's case?"

She hears a female voice in the background: "George? Who is it?"

"It's all right, honey," he says, then to Sykes, "My wife, Kim." Then back to his wife, "I'll just be a minute, honey." Then to Sykes, "I know he tried hard, probably too hard. Was downright territorial about it, and I kind of blame him for it not going anywhere. You know, the case of his career, him not sharing information, working in secret. I bet you're familiar with things like that."

"'Fraid so."

"As best I recall, he seemed to have this notion he was onto something, hot on the trail, wouldn't say just what that trail was, guess nobody else knew what it was, either.

That's probably one reason it never got solved. That's always been my belief."

Sykes thinks of the calls made from Barber's home phone. Maybe that's the explanation. He was secretive, didn't want any dispatchers or his fellow investigators to catch the scent of what he was following. Maybe Barber wanted to solve the case himself, didn't want to share the glory. Yes, she's all too familiar with that MO.

"Honey," George is talking to his wife again, clearly trying to soothe her. "Why don't you go make us some coffee? It's all right." Back to Sykes. "Kim took it the hardest, was as close to my aunt as a daughter. Oh Lord, I hate all this has to come up." He keeps sighing.

Sykes questions him a little further. George was in his early forties when his aunt was murdered, is the son of her only sibling, Edmund Finlay, and when Sykes tries to make sense of how George and his aunt could have the same last name, he explains that she was quite strong-willed, proud of her distinguished family name, and refused to give it up when she married. George is an only child. He and his wife, Kim, have two grown children who live out west, the couple spend all of their time in Flat Rock, left Tennessee for good not long after the murder, just couldn't be there anymore, couldn't handle the memories, especially Kim couldn't, practically had a nervous breakdown afterward.

Sykes promises to get back with him or, more likely, an investigator named Winston Garano will. George doesn't sound very happy when he hears that part.

"It's just awfully painful to open up all this," he explains. "You mind my asking why it's necessary after all these years?"

"We're just looking into a few things, sir. I appreciate your cooperation."

"Of course. Whatever I can do to help."

He'd rather eat dirt than help, Sykes thinks. When the anger goes away and the ugliness fades, a lot of people don't care about justice anymore. They just want to forget.

"Too bad," she mutters to Barber's dark, wretched basement. *It's not like I'm having fun, either.*

She ponders and contemplates, perched on the pickle bucket like that statue *The Thinker,* resumes going through more bills, finds a MasterCard bill for September, pulls out what is in the envelope, finds something that gives her a disk error, as she calls it.

"What the hell?" she mutters, staring at a document with a cover sheet stamped with an autopsy case number, then another case number, this one a police file number sloppily scribbled in pencil: KPD893-85.

The page underneath it is a medical examiner's inventory of Vivian Finlay's personal effects, and stapled to it is a Polaroid photograph of mutilated male body parts, grimy and gory: feet, arms and legs, pieces and parts, guts, a decapitated head, arranged on top of a steel autopsy table covered with a green sheet. The case number written on a six-inch ruler used as a reference scale indicates that the death occurred in North Carolina in 1983.

Win wakes up with a start, for an instant not sure where he is. He realizes he's been asleep for more than two hours, still in his clothes, his neck stiff, the coffee on his bedside table cold.

He checks his phone messages, skipping over the earlier ones left by Sykes when he was too busy with Lamont to deal with the

Finlay case. Sykes has left him another message: She's sent him files over the Internet and he needs to look at them right away and call her. His computer is neatly centered on a Stickley desk (yard sale), and he sits down, enters Sykes's number, gets her on her cell phone.

"Good God!" She hurts his ear. "I just heard!"

"Whoa," he says. "You near a landline?"

She gives him a number he recognizes as the Academy. He calls her back.

"Good God!" she starts in again. "It's all over the news. Good God, Win! What happened?"

"I'll tell you about it later, Sykes."

"You get in a shootout and you're going to tell me later? At least you killed him. Goddamn, and her. How's that gonna work? The DA? That's all anybody's talking about down here."

"Can we move on, Sykes?"

"The part I don't get is how you ended up at her house, walked right into it. She invite you there for a nightcap or something?"

It doesn't take a detective to pick up on her jealousy. The beautiful, powerful Lamont, all the more formidable because Sykes has never met her, and now she imagines him heroically saving her life, probably thinks Lamont is devoted to him forever, wants to quit her job for him, get married, have his children, throw herself on a funeral pyre when he dies.

"Tell me what you've got," he says. "You find the file?"

"After spending half the night in Barber's damn basement, everything but."

He sips his cold coffee, goes into his e-mail, sees files from her, converts them to documents as she talks fast, hardly takes a breath, tells him about MasterCard and phone bills, about Barber's probable territoriality and glory-hunting and secrecy, what Mrs. Finlay's nephew had to say. Then gets to the part about some man who had a bad encounter with a train in Charlotte two years before Mrs. Finlay's murder.

"Whoa, slow down," Win interrupts her, scanning a document on his screen. "What's a train death got to do with anything?"

"You tell me. You looking at the picture?"

"Looking at it now." He studies the photograph on his screen, not very good quality, a Polaroid of raggedly severed limbs and intestines and chunks of flesh piled next to a mutilated torso and severed head, what looks like black grease and dirt everywhere. White guy. Black hair. Pretty young, as best Win can tell. "You checked it out with the ME's office?"

"You know, I didn't realize this was my case."

His cell phone rings. He doesn't answer, impatiently silences it.

"Hey," Win says to Sykes. "You sound pissed at me."

"I'm not pissed at you," Sykes says angrily.

"Good. Because I've got plenty of people pissed at me and don't need you added to the list."

"Like who?"

"Her, for starters."

"You mean after what you did . . . ?"

"Exactly. I've tried to tell you. She's borderline, a sociopath, Bonnie without Clyde, doesn't need a Clyde, thinks all of us are Clydes. Hates Clydes, actually."

"You saying Lamont doesn't like men?"

"Not sure she likes anybody."

"Well, it'd be nice if you'd say thanks." Sykes tries to sound gruff. "I've been up all night running down crap for you, and I'm supposed to be in class in five minutes and where am I? In the damn media room sending files to you, trying to call people, mostly getting cussed at. I'm going to look at the case later today, on a flight to Raleigh, the ME's office in Chapel Hill."

"Who *cussed* at you?" He smiles a little. When she gets riled, she sounds like a little kid, one as Southern as pecan pie.

"Some damn Charlotte cop. And who's going to reimburse me for my plane ticket, by the way?"

"Don't worry. I'll take care of everything," he says, scrolling through another file, information that came from Detective Barber's basement, puzzled by a medical examiner's inventory of personal effects removed from a dead body in the morgue. "What did the *damn Charlotte cop* who worked the train fatality have to say?"

One pair of ruffled blue tennis panties with ball pocket, he reads the inventory.

One Izod white tennis skirt and matching shirt, bloody . . .

His cell phone rings again. He ignores it.

"The big jerk." Sykes continues to vent all over the map. "He's the police chief now, you know what they say about what floats to the top."

He zooms in on a number written in pencil on the upper-right corner of the personal effects report.

KPD893-85.

"Sykes?"

". . . Said I'd have to submit my request in writing if I want copies of the reports, which by now would probably be on microfilm," she is saying. "But he said he didn't understand the interest, there was nothing to it . . ."

"Sykes? KPD893-85. Vivian Finlay? She was wearing tennis clothes when she was murdered?"

"Try telling that to him, the guy smashed to smithereens by the damn freight train. *Nothing to it . . .*"

"Sykes! This inventory is Vivian Finlay's personal effects when she came into the morgue?"

"That's the next bizarre part, the only thing I could find from her case file. Where the hell's the rest of it?"

"These bloody tennis clothes are what's been in the Knoxville PD's evidence room for twenty years, what's being tested for DNA in California?"

The autopsy report Lamont gave him depicts a tiny seventy-three-year-old lady.

"You sure this personal-effects form is from her case?" Win asks.

"That's her case number for sure. I looked at every damn thing in every damn box while that Roller Derby drunk wife of his rattled around in the kitchen upstairs, stomped around, made sure I knew how unwelcome I was. There's nothing else."

He looks at the personal-effects inventory again, realizes something he should have noticed immediately.

"Her nephew says he'll be glad to talk to us," Sykes says. "Well, not *glad*. But he will."

"Size ten," Win says as someone knocks on the door. "The tennis clothes are size ten. A five-foot, ninety-one-pound woman doesn't wear size ten. Now what!" as the knocking becomes more insistent.

"Got to go," he tells Sykes, gets up from his desk, walks into his living room as the urgent knocking continues.

He looks through the peephole, sees

Sammy's flushed, unhappy face, opens the door.

"I've been trying to get you for a damn hour," Sammy blurts out.

"How'd you know I was here?" Win asks, confused, his mind going everywhere.

"I'm a detective. Your home phone's busy. She just screeched at me like an air-raid siren."

"Who?"

"Who do you think. You got to come with me right now. She's waiting for you at the *Globe*."

"Forget it," Win says.

8

Stuart Hamilton, the managing editor, main-
tains his appropriate demeanor as he sits
inside his office with Lamont and a senior
reporter and a photographer. The office is
glass. Everyone in the newsroom is witness
to what no doubt will be an unprecedented
interview, maybe the biggest news in the
city since the Red Sox won the World Se-
ries.

Everyone, and there must be a hundred
people beyond the glass, can see the well-
known, formidable DA Monique Lamont, in a
dark warm-up suit, exhausted, no makeup,
sitting on a sofa, their commander in chief,

Hamilton, listening, nodding, his face somber. Journalists, secretaries, editors are guarded in their glances from the other side of the glass, but Lamont knows she is being watched, talked about, that looks are being exchanged, that e-mails are firing from desk to desk. It is what she wants. The interview will run on A1, above the fold. It will race through cyberspace and land in papers and on Internet news sites all around the world. It will be talked about on television, the radio.

Crawley can go to hell.

"Because I have no choice," she is saying from the sofa, her shoes off, her legs curled under her as if she is having coffee with old friends. "I owe it to women everywhere." She catches herself. "To men, women, children, all victimized people everywhere."

Careful. Don't suggest that sexual violence is a problem restricted to women. Don't refer to yourself as a victim.

"If we are going to destigmatize sexual violence. Pedophilia. Rape—and not only women are raped—" she continues, "then we must be open about it and speak of it in the context of violence and not simply in the context of sex."

"So you're basically desexualizing it at the

same time you're demythologizing it," the reporter says, Pascal Plasser-something, she never can get his name right.

Last time he interviewed her, he was reasonably fair, reasonably truthful, and not particularly bright, which is why she requested him when she showed up unannounced at the newspaper, rang Hamilton, told him that if he assured her the coverage she deserves for an exclusive of this magnitude, she would talk openly about what just happened.

"No, Pascal," she says. "That's not what I'm doing at all."

She wonders where Win is and her anger spikes, fear sits in her stomach like lead.

She says, "I can't possibly desexualize what happened to me. It was a sexual crime. Sexual violence that could have exacted the ultimate price. My life."

"It's incredibly courageous for you to do this, Monique," Hamilton says with an air of solemnity, of sorrow, like he's a damn funeral home director. "But I must point out that some of your detractors will view this as a political ploy. Governor Crawley, for example . . ."

"A *ploy*?" She leans forward on the sofa,

holds Hamilton's gaze. "Someone puts a gun to my head, ties me up, rapes me with the intention of murdering me and burning down my house, and that's a *ploy*?"

"Your talking about it might be construed as . . ."

"Stuart," she says, and her mettle, her self-control are remarkable. "I welcome anybody to suggest such a thing. I challenge them. I dare them."

She's not quite sure how she can be so poised, and a part of her is terrified that it isn't normal for her to be this pulled together, that maybe it's the dead calm before a horrific storm, the sane moment before the strait- jacket or suicide.

"Why do you say you'd welcome it?" Pascal What's-his-name asks, scribbling notes, flipping a page.

"Anybody," she says ominously. "*Anybody* who says or suggests such a thing will only succeed in revealing his true character. Good. Let him try."

"Him?"

"Let anybody try."

She looks through the glass, surveys the expanse of bleak partitioned space, journalists in their cubicles, rodents who feed on the garbage and tragedies of others. She looks for Win, waits for his formidable, striking presence to suddenly dominate the newsroom, striding her way. But there is no sign of him, and her hope begins to fade. Anger flares.

He has defied her directive. He has degraded her, belittled her, shown his misogynistic contempt.

"Your new crime initiative—in fact published in this very paper this morning—*any crime, any time,*" Hamilton says. "What might you say now?

"And will this new cold-case initiative, At Risk, the murder in Tennessee, somehow take a backseat to . . . ?"

Win isn't coming. She'll punish him for this.

"I couldn't be more motivated and determined to bring about justice in any violent crime, no matter how long ago it was committed," Lamont says. "In fact, I've assigned Investigator Garano to At Risk full-time while he's on leave from my Middlesex County headquarters."

"Leave? So there's a question about whether the shooting of Roger Baptista was merited?" Pascal is suddenly alert, more alert than he has been throughout her brave, painful interview.

"Any time deadly force is used, no matter the apparent circumstances," Lamont says, placing emphasis on the word *apparent,* "we must investigate the incident to the fullest."

"Are you implying that the force might have been excessive?"

"I can make no further comment at this time," she says.

Win feels a little guilty walking into the state police crime laboratory with his sealed envelope, knowing it really isn't fair to bypass backlogs and protocols when he wants evidence analyzed right away.

He doesn't feel the least bit guilty for not showing up at the *Globe* to further Lamont's relentless political aspirations, to participate in behavior that is inappropriate, outrageous, and, in his opinion, self-destructive. Sammy says her *exclusive tell-all* is already being talked about in cyberspace, on TV and the radio, getting everybody primed to read her prurient and pitiful interview. He has decided she's reckless and irrational, and that's not a good thing if the person is your boss.

The modern brick building with its heavy steel front doors is a haven for Win, a place to go when he wants to unload on Captain Jessie Huber, discuss cases, complain, confide, ask for advice, maybe a favor or two. Win walks through the green and blue glass-block lobby, heads down a long hall-way, and helps himself to the familiar open door where he finds his friend and mentor, typically dapper in a conservative dark suit and a gray silk cravat, typically on the phone. Huber is tall and thin, bald as a full moon, and women find him sexy, maybe because he is formidable and a good lis-tener. Three years ago he was the senior in-vestigator in Win's unit, then was appointed to take over the labs.

He hangs up when he sees Win, bolts up from his desk, blurts out, "Dammit, boy!" and hugs him the way men hug, more back-slapping than anything else. "Sit, sit! I can't believe it. Tell me what the hell's going on." He shuts the door, pulls a chair close. "I send you to Tennessee, best damn forensic training facility on the planet, right up your alley. Then what? What the hell you doing back up here and what the hell have you gotten yourself into?"

"You sent me?" Win sits, puzzled. "Thought it was Lamont. Thought it was her brilliant brainstorm to send me to the Academy, maybe so she could have me handy to work a *small-town case,* as she views it, that would make all us *big-city folks* up here look good."

Huber pauses, as if considering what he's going to say next, then, "You just killed somebody, Win. Let's don't talk politics."

"I killed somebody because of politics. Politics are why I was ordered back up here to have dinner with her, Jessie."

"I understand."

"I'm glad somebody does."

"You're very angry."

"I'm being used. Given nothing to work with. Can't even find the damn case file."

"Looks like you and me share the same opinion of this At Risk mess she's gotten us into," Huber says.

"I thought it was the governor's initiative, that she's just the quarterback. That's how it was explained. . . ."

"Yes and no," Huber interrupts, leaning forward in his chair, lowering his voice. "This is all about her. She cooked it up, suggested it to Crawley, convinced him it would make the Commonwealth, make him look good. She might get most valuable player, but he's the team owner, right? Not hard to talk a governor, especially Crawley, into something like this—you know how out of touch governors can be when it comes to minutiae. What do you mean you can't find the case file?"

"Just what I said. The Finlay police case file—gone. Lost in space."

Huber gets a disgusted look on his face, almost rolls his eyes, mutters, "Jesus, wouldn't you suppose she would have had it sent to her office?" He picks up the phone, dials, glances up at him, adds, "Before she dragged you into this?"

"She says . . ." Win starts to reply.

"Hey," Huber says to the person who answers the phone. "I got Win Garano here with me. The Finlay case file. You ever see it?" A pause, then Huber stares at Win, says, "No big surprise. Thanks," and hangs up.

"What?" Win asks, a bad feeling fluttering in his stomach.

"Toby says he got it weeks ago, put it on Lamont's desk."

"She told me she's never seen it. Knoxville PD's never seen it, either. How 'bout giving me Toby's phone number."

Did Lamont lie? Did she lose the file? Did somebody take it before she ever saw it?

"Politics, my boy." Huber is saying. "Maybe dirty politics," he emphasizes with an ominous look in his eyes, writes down a phone number, hands it to him. "When she first told me about At Risk, I was emphatic she should never have talked Crawley into it and should try to talk him out of it. *Any crime, any time.* Jesus. What? We start doing DNA testing on every unsolved violent crime since the Great Flood? Meanwhile, we've got a backlog of some five hundred cases. Real cases with real people out there raping, killing."

"I'm not sure I understand why you would send me to Knoxville." Win can't get past that, feels shaky, a little dazed.

"Thought I was doing you a service. Great place and great on your résumé."

"I know you've always looked out for me . . . but it just seems coincidental I'm down there and then . . . ."

"Look. It's coincidental to a point," Huber says. "Lamont was determined to work an old case that wasn't local. You happened to be in Tennessee, Win, and happened to be the investigator she wanted involved."

"What if I hadn't been in Tennessee?"

"She would have found some other old case in some other distant town and probably loaned you out one way or another. You know, us enlightened New Englanders to the rescue," he adds sarcastically. "Send in the Yankee troops from the land of MIT and Harvard. Easy to bury, too, right? If things don't go so well down there in some quaint little Southern town, eventually—maybe even by election time—everyone up here forgets about it. Lot harder to bury some cold-case homicide that might have happened in Massachusetts, right?"

"Probably."

Huber leans back in his chair, adds, "I hear you're the star down there at the Academy."

Win doesn't reply, his thoughts stuck in multiple places. He's sweating under his suit, a cold sweat.

"Your future, Win. I don't think you want to work for her the rest of your life or run around all hours of the day and night working misdemeanor murders, one scumbag killing another. Not to mention the money. I sure as hell got tired of it. Training. The best. Grooming. You're so damn talented. I'm thinking you'll be replacing me as lab director when I retire, and I'm counting the days. All depending on the powers to be, who the governor is." He gets a knowing look on his face. "You following me?"

Win isn't following much. Stays silent, has a feeling about Huber. One he's never felt before.

"You trust me?"

"Always have," Win replies.

"You trust me now?" Huber says, his face very serious.

Win won't go there, says, "Trust you enough to spend my mental-health day with you, Jessie. That's the way we do things here in the land of Oz when we kill somebody on the job. How 'bout it?"

"I'm not in the stress unit anymore, my good friend. You know that."

"Doesn't matter. And you know that. I'm declaring this an official counseling session with the experienced counselor of my choice. Anybody inquires, I just had my mental-health day. Go on, ask me how I feel."

"Tell me."

"Regretful that deadly force was necessary," Win mechanically recites. "All broken up about it, can't sleep. Did everything I could to stop him, but he left me no choice. It's tragic. Just a kid, maybe he could have been rehabilitated, added something positive to society."

Huber stares at him for a long moment, then, "I'm gonna throw up."

"All right then. Grateful he didn't kill Lamont. Or me. Angry the worthless piece of shit did this to her, to me. Glad he's dead so he doesn't sue me. You mind if I borrow Rake for a little while?" Win holds up the envelope, the back of it sealed with yellow evidence tape initialed by him. "Maybe try out her ESDA magic box or that fancy image-enhancement software you just got or both on a letter? Reminds me, any prints on the money, the thousand dollars in Baptista's pocket?"

"Already ran them in IAFIS. Nothing." Huber gets up, goes back behind his desk, sits in his swivel chair.

"You got any thoughts about it?" Win then says. "Robbery gone bad or something else?"

Huber hesitates, says, "Enemies? The list

is long, Win. I think by now you're seeing the scary truth for yourself, and I'd be very careful what you tell her, what you ask her, very, very careful. A shame. A damn shame, because you know what? She wasn't like that when she got started, was a real ball-buster, took down a lot of dirtbags, had my respect. Let's just put it this way, the word *ethics* probably isn't in her fancy vocabulary anymore."

"I thought the two of you were buddies. Here she's doing this little favor for your son."

"Right, buddies." He smiles ruefully. "In this business, never let people know what you really think of them. She certainly has no clue what Toby really thinks of her."

"Or you?"

"Incompetent and blames everything on everybody else, including Toby. Two guys talking? Between you and me, Geronimo? She's going down," Huber says. "It's really sad."

9

The forensic pathologist who conducted the autopsy on the train fatality died one week later during a Sunday afternoon of skydiving when his parachute didn't open.

If Sykes didn't have the original case file in front of her, she might not believe it. *Bad karma,* she thinks uncomfortably. As a kid, she loved archaeology. It was one of the few subjects that interested her, maybe because it wasn't taught in school. She lost interest when she read about King Tut's tomb, about curses and people mysteriously dying.

"Twenty years ago, Mrs. Finlay's death,"

she is saying to Win over the phone. "Two years before that a train death, then the ME's death. I'm getting a little freaked out."

"Possibly coincidence," he says.

"Then why was the picture stapled to Mrs. Finlay's personal-effects inventory?"

"Maybe we shouldn't talk about this right now," says Win, who doesn't like cell phones and certainly doesn't assume that any conversation on them is secure.

Sykes is alone in the small morgue office on the eleventh floor of a tall, beige building behind the UNC–Chapel Hill medical school's hospitals. She is bewildered, seems the more she looks into Vivian Finlay's violent death, the more mysterious it gets. First, her case file has disappeared except for an inventory of clothing she supposedly had on when she was murdered, tennis clothes that would appear to be the wrong size. Second, a train fatality may somehow be connected to her case, and now the ME and his skydiving accident.

"Just a few things," Win adds. "Keep the details to a minimum. How?"

"Chute didn't open."

"There should have been an autopsy on the chute."

"How about I e-mail all this to you," Sykes says. "How about you read it yourself. When you getting back this way?"

She's feeling very isolated, abandoned. He's up there with that DA, the two of them headline news. As far as Sykes is concerned, he was involved in a shooting, should get out of town and be down here to help her out. It's his case. Well, that's not how it's feeling anymore. But the fact is, it's his case. Typically, now that something sensational has happened, an old lady murdered twenty years ago is a throwaway. Who cares.

"As soon as I can," is all Win has to say about it.

"I know you got some real problems up there," she replies as reasonably as possible. "But this is your case, Win. And if I don't get back to the Academy, the TBI will be all over me like white on rice."

"Whatever happens, I'll fix it," he says.

He always promises that and so far he hasn't fixed a damn thing. She spends all her time talking to him, doesn't study or hang out with the other students discussing what they just learned that day in class, then gets behind and doesn't fully comprehend the newest forensic technology and investigative techniques or have friends. She complains and he says, *Don't worry. You got me and I'm a great tutor.* She says maybe she shouldn't devote so much of herself to a man almost young enough to be her son, and he says he doesn't care about age, then pays attention to some younger woman or obsesses about that DA, Lamont, who's smart and beautiful, well, maybe damaged goods now. Not nice to think it, but a lot of men don't want a woman after she's been raped.

Sykes goes through the medical examiner's case. His name was Dr. Hurt. That figures, might be funny if it wasn't so sad. Fell from an estimated five thousand feet, she reads, suffered massive trauma to his head, part of his brain avulsed, femurs driven up into his hips, crushed and fractured this, ruptured that. The only mention of the parachute is a brief description by a police officer who responded to the scene. He stated it appeared the chute was improperly packed. Witnesses claimed Dr. Hurt packed it himself. The possibility was raised that he might have committed suicide.

Colleagues and family acknowledged he

was deeply in debt and getting divorced but claimed he wasn't depressed or acting oddly at all—in fact, seemed to be in good spirits. Sykes has heard that tall tale before, people didn't notice a thing. Well guess why. If they admit there was even the slightest reason for concern, they might feel guilty about being so caught up in their own lives that they couldn't take a moment to worry about somebody else. She looks up as a knock sounds and the door opens. The chief medical examiner walks in, a mousy kind of pinched-looking woman somewhere in her fifties, granny glasses, a loose lab coat, a stethoscope around her neck.

"Now that's something," Sykes says, looking pointedly at the stethoscope. "You making sure everybody's dead before you start cutting and sawing?"

The chief smiles, says, "My secretary asked me to check her lungs. She's getting bronchitis. Just making sure you don't need anything."

It's more than that.

"I don't guess you were around here when Dr. Hurt died," Sykes says.

"I succeeded him. What's this about, exactly? Why all the interest?" She glances at the two case files on the table.

Sykes isn't going to tell her, says, "Several seemingly unrelated deaths may have something in common. You know how it is, you have to look at everything."

"I think it was pretty clear he was a suicide. Why's the TBI involved?"

"It's not, exactly."

"Then you're not working the case?" she interrupts.

"I'm helping. It's not my case." As if Sykes needs to be reminded of that one more time. "Like I said, I'm just checking out a few things."

"Well, I see. I guess it's all right. I'll be in the morgue if you need me," the chief says, and she shuts the door behind her.

Guess it's all right. As if Sykes is a Girl Scout.

Then she thinks about Dr. Hurt, wonders about his state of mind, his level of professional competence, the effort he put forth if he was anxious and depressed and no longer valued his life. She imagines herself in a similar situation and is fairly certain she would miss important details, might not try very hard, maybe wouldn't care. She keeps that in mind as she reviews the train fatality, a terribly mutilating death that occurred at a rail crossing on a two-lane rural highway, the freight train's engineer stating that when he rounded a sharp curve at approximately eight fifteen that morning, he saw the decedent lying facedown across the tracks and couldn't stop the train in time to avoid running over him. The victim's name was Mark Holland, a thirty-nine-year-old detective with the Asheville Police Department.

His widow, Kimberly, was quoted in the newspaper as saying that her husband left their Asheville home early the previous evening en route to Charlotte, where he was to meet with someone, she didn't know who, but "it was related to work." He was not depressed and she could think of no reason whatsoever to account for his alleged suicide, that she was extremely upset and adamant that he would not have done such a thing, especially since "he just got promoted and we were excited about starting a family."

The autopsy revealed a laceration to Mark Holland's head and an underlying fracture (*Well, no friggin' wonder*) that was *consistent with a fall.*

Dr. Hurt wasn't just depressed, Sykes thinks, he was lights on, nobody home, bought into the Charlotte cop's suggestion that Holland was crossing the railroad tracks on foot, perhaps on his way to have a secret meeting with a witness, tripped, fell, knocked himself unconscious. Dr. Hurt signed out the case as an accident.

Forensic scientist Rachael—or "Rake," as Win calls her—places the letter on top of a porous metal platen called a vacuum bed. She hits a switch and begins vacuuming down the box.

He has watched her work the electrostatic imaging system before, and sometimes they've been lucky, most recently in a kidnapping case, the ransom note written on a sheet of paper that obviously had been under one the kidnapper had used earlier to jot down a phone number that led the police to a Papa John's Pizza where he had placed a take-out order and paid for it with a credit card. Rake wears white cotton examination gloves, was happy when Win told her he hadn't touched the letter with his bare hands. After they've finished looking for indented writing, the letter the man in the red scarf left for Win at the Diesel Café will go to the fingerprints lab to be processed with ninhydrin or some other reagent.

"How's Knoxville?" asks Rake, a nice-looking brunette who started out with the FBI lab in Quantico but decided after 9-11 and the Patriot Act that she didn't want to work for the Feds. "You gonna start talking with a dueling-banjo twang?"

"That's North Georgia, *Deliverance* country. No dueling banjos in Knoxville, just blaze-orange everywhere."

"Hunting?"

"UT football."

Rake covers the letter and the platen with a clear plastic imaging film that reminds Win of Saran Wrap.

"Win?" she says without looking up. "Sounds trite, but I'm sorry about what happened."

"Thanks, Rake."

She passes what she calls a corona discharge unit over the surface. Win always smells ozone when she does it, as if it might rain.

"I don't care what anybody says. You did

the right thing," she adds. "I don't see how anybody can even question it."

"I didn't realize anybody was," he says, getting one of his uneasy feelings.

She tilts the tray and cascades toner-coated beads over the image film–covered document, says, "Heard it on the radio during a coffee break."

The electrostatic charge causes the toner to migrate to indentations that aren't visible to the unaided eye, areas of the paper with microscopic damage caused by handwriting.

"Go on. Tell me," Win says, already knows.

He's being screwed.

"Just that Lamont said you're being investigated, like maybe it wasn't a good shooting. A big story's being run tomorrow and they're already promoting it with teases." She looks at him, adds, "How's that for grateful?"

"Maybe what I expected," he says as latent images appear in faint black, partial words, confusing.

Rake isn't impressed, points out something on the threatening letter the man in the red scarf left for Win, decides, "Think we'd better try three-D enhancement."

Toby Huber is cold, shivering as he sits on his balcony of the Winnetu Inn in South Beach, Edgartown, smoking a joint, looking at the ocean, at people in long pants and jackets walking along the beach.

"I'm sure it's gone, just not where, exactly," he says over his cell phone, annoyed but with a nice buzz going. "Sorry, man. But at this point, it doesn't matter."

"That's not for you to judge. Try to think for once."

"Look. I told you, okay? It must be when I threw out everything in trash bags, whatever. And I mean everything, including any food in the fridge, any beer, anything. Even hauled the trash about five miles away to a Dumpster behind . . . some restaurant, can't remember which one. Damn it's freezing here. I've checked and rechecked and it's not here. Man, you need to chill before you have a stroke. . . ."

A knock from inside the one-bedroom suite, and then the door opens, the housekeeper is startled as Toby steps inside and glares at her.

"What is it you don't understand about *Do Not Disturb*!" he screams at her.

"Sorry, sir. The card's not on the door." She quickly vanishes.

Toby returns to the balcony, takes a toke, almost yells into the phone, "I'm out of here. You got that? Where it's warm. Boring as goddamn hell here. You've put me through enough and it'd better be worth it."

"Not quite yet. It will look suspicious if you're suddenly flying off to L.A. You need to stay put a few more days. We've got to make sure it's not someplace where it might be found and cause us a lot of trouble. Think, Toby!"

"If it's anywhere, it's still inside the damn apartment. I don't know. . . ." Something glimmers. He's not sure he checked under the bed, mentions that, adding, "You know, when I was reading it, could have stuck it there. Why don't you go check your goddamn self?"

"I already have."

"Then you're so spazzed out about it, go check again!"

"Think! Where did you have it last? You sure you didn't leave it at the office. . . ."

"I told you. I took it with me, know that for fact because I was reading it."

"I didn't tell you to take it so you could read it!"

"Yeah, so you've said about a hundred times by now, so you can just shut up about it, okay?"

"You put it in your car, drove it there? What? Reading it in bed? So you could look at the damn pictures? Are you insane! Where did you have it last!"

"I told you to shut up, don't act like such a hysterical old woman. It's not like I can exactly go look. So you help yourself, look 'til the cows come home. Maybe I missed it, okay? I had it all kinds of places when I was there. In a drawer, maybe in a pile by the bed, under the pillow. At one point I had it in a basket of dirty clothes. Or maybe it was in the dryer. . . ."

"Toby, are you sure you didn't take it with you to the Vineyard?"

"How many times you going to ask me! What difference does it make. So what if it's gone? Nothing worked the way it was supposed to, anyway."

"Well, we don't *know* it's gone, now do we? And that's a problem, a very serious problem. You were supposed to leave it where it would be found. The last thing you did before you left. But you didn't. You completely ignored my orders."

"So it probably ended up in the trash, okay? That's probably what happened when I cleaned things out." He takes another toke. "You know, it's not like I didn't have a lot on my mind, right? And he kept wanting to know about the money, said I'd better give it to him in advance, and I said half of it up front, and then you took forever getting it for me. . . ."

"How the hell did I end up with someone like you?"

Holding in smoke. Exhaling. "Because you're lucky. So far. But that can change, you know."

Rake is lost in a software world of pixels and Z ranges and histograms, panning, zooming, rotating, manipulating light angles, surface reflection, contour enhancement while Win stares at the big flat screen, looking at shadowy shapes in magnified 3-D.

He starts seeing a word, maybe numbers.

"An *e,* an *r,* a *w,* lowercase?" he suggests. "And three and ninety-six?"

There's more. She keeps working, the words and numbers materializing. Odd-looking, almost overlaid.

"More than one note that's left indented writing?" Win considers.

"That's what I'm thinking," Rake says. "Could very well be indentations from different writings on different sheets from the same pad of paper. You know, you write a note, then another page down, write another one, and the pressure of the pen or pencil pressed against the paper is sufficiently strong to create an indented image multiple sheets down."

She works some more and they make out what they can: *three-year market exclusivity,* and *okay,* and partly overlaying that, suggesting it was a separate writing on a separate sheet of paper, is *$8.96* and what appears to be *up from an earlier forecast of $6.11.*

10

Monique Lamont sits in a marble and cherry kitchen on Mount Vernon Street in Beacon Hill, one of the most expensive and coveted addresses in Boston. She is drinking her first martini of the day, straight up, Grey Goose, one pimiento-stuffed green olive, and a glass that she took out of the freezer.

She wears jeans and a loose-fitting denim shirt. The warm-up suit she had on earlier is in the Dumpster behind the nineteenth-century brick complex where the apartment was safely and secretly tucked away until this morning when Sammy disclosed the location to the troops, insisting that the police patrol the area, insisting that she can't stay in her Cambridge house, not now, not that she would. She will always see the back door, the key box, the gas can. She will always see him in her bedroom, the gun pointed at her head as he did what he wanted, as he re-created her into his own image—a small, filthy creature, a nothing, a nobody.

"I only wish I'd killed him myself," she says.

Huber sits across the table from her, drinking his second beer. He is having a hard time looking at her, his gaze interrupted as if his eye muscles are suddenly palsied.

"You've got to get beyond this, Monique," he says. "I know that's easy for me to say. But you're not thinking right, couldn't possibly be under the circumstances."

"Shut up, Jessie. If it ever happens to you, you'll find yourself howling at the damn moon. Then you'll understand empathy."

"So it helps if you ruin everything else in your life? You shouldn't have told them about this place."

"And what? Refuse police protection when I don't know who's behind what happened, who put him up to it?"

"We don't know for a fact that anybody did."

"Go to a hotel? Walk into the lobby, find the media in packs, waiting to tear into me?"

"You're the one who went to the media," he says somberly, his eyes moving around, doing their cold, calculating thing. "Now we have to take your crap and make caviar out of it."

He has the worst metaphors and analogies of anyone Lamont has ever met. She says, "Why did you let him? You could have told him the documents lab was tied up, that Rachael wasn't there, was busy, something. That was stupid, Jessie."

"Win's always had a special membership to Club Crime Lab. He's too smart. If I'd started making excuses, he would have known right away something was going on. He trusts me like a father."

"Then he's not as smart as you think." She sips her martini, drains the glass, eats the olive.

"And you're a Harvard snob." Huber gets up, opens the freezer, gets out the Grey Goose, a frozen glass, makes her another, forgets the olive.

She stares at the martini he sets on the table, stares at it long enough for him to remember the olive.

"You know what that guy's IQ is?" Huber says from inside the refrigerator. "Higher than yours and mine put together."

She replays that unforgiving footage, Win seeing her, handing her his jacket, telling her to take deep breaths. She sees him seeing her naked and powerless and degraded.

"He just can't take tests, the damndest thing," Huber continues, opens another beer. "Graduated from high school with a four-point-oh, valedictorian, most likely to succeed, best-looking, best everything except for one minor thing. Tanked his SATs. Then, after college, tanked his GREs, his LSATs. He can't take tests. Something happens to him."

Win didn't show up at the *Globe*. He defied her. He has no respect for her after seeing her . . .

"I hear there are people like that." Huber sits back down. "Brilliant but can't take tests."

"I'm not interested in his learning disabilities," Lamont says. "What exactly did he find out at the lab?" The vodka has made her tongue bigger, less nimble, her thoughts stuttering. "Or what does he think he found out?"

"He probably doesn't know what it means. Can't prove anything, anyway."

"That's not what I asked!"

"Notes from a phone conversation with my broker."

"Oh God."

"Don't worry. They won't find fingerprints, nothing to link that letter to me. One thing I do know is forensic science." He smiles. "Win probably thinks it's you. For that matter, probably thinks you're behind it. Probably thinks Roy did it, called him a *half-breed*." Huber laughs. "Now that for sure pissed him off."

"Another one of your impulsive, high risk decisions."

He didn't ask her, just did it. Then he told her after the fact because the more she knows, the more implicated she is, that's been his strategy all along.

"It did exactly what I said it would." Huber drinks his beer. "You threaten him, insult him, try to scare him off a case, and he locks his jaws on it like a pit bull."

She is silent, sips her martini, trapped.

She says, "It wasn't necessary. He's a pit bull anyway."

"Your fault for insisting on talking to him in person instead of over the phone. You should have left him down there in Knoxville." He pauses, his face twitching. "Maybe you got a thing about him. That's what it looks like."

"Go to hell, Jessie."

"Of course, it's a blessing he was here. Providence, your guardian angel, living right, whatever," he indelicately, indifferently goes on. "Win got pissed and came to see you. As it turns out, my little ploy actually did us all quite a favor. You're still alive, Monique."

"Don't sound so disappointed."

"Monique . . ."

"I'm not joking." She holds his gaze, doesn't flinch, realizes she has come to hate him, to wish him harm, misery, poverty, death. Then, "I don't want Toby coming back. He's worthless. I'm done with that favor. I'm done with any favors."

"He can't stand working for you anyway."

"I've had enough of you, Jessie. I have for a long time." The vodka is making her uninhibited. He can go to hell. "I told you I'm not playing along with it anymore. I goddamn meant it. It's not worth it."

"Of course it is. You've gotten what you want, Monique. What you deserve," he says, and there is no mistaking what he means.

She stares at him, shocked. "What I deserve?"

He stares back at her.

"I deserve *that*? You're saying I deserve *that*! You bastard!"

"I meant you work hard, should get something for it." His eyes don't jump around this time. They look at her, flat, nothing in them.

She starts to cry.

It is dark now, the moon new.

Win opens the driver's door of Nana's old Buick, stopped in the middle of the road again, watching Miss Dog wandering aimlessly again, headlights flashing in her old, blind eyes.

"That's it. The end," Win says, furious. "Come here, girl," he coaxes, whistling. "Come on, Miss Dog. What'cha doing on the street again, huh? She forget to shut the door? Let you out, her fat ass too lazy to make sure you got back in? Her son-in-law lowlife kick you again?"

Miss Dog's tail droops, her head hangs. She drops to her belly as if she's done something wrong. Win gently picks her up, keeps talking, wonders if she can hear him at all, places her inside the car, drives off, tells her where she's going and what will happen next. Maybe she hears him, maybe she doesn't. She licks his hand. He parks behind Nana's house, and the wind chimes are chiming softly, the night clear, the cool air barely stirring, the chimes quietly chiming as if telling secrets, and he unlocks the back door, Miss Dog draped over his shoulder like a furry sack of potatoes.

"Nana?"

He follows the sound of the TV.

"Nana? We have a new addition to the family."

Sykes has been on the phone for more than an hour, getting bounced from one old-timer to the next. Twenty-three years ago is forever. So far, no one at the Asheville Police Department remembers Detective Mark Holland.

She dials another number as she drives

west toward Knoxville, approaching headlights confusing her, reminding her what a
rip-off it is to get old. She can't see worth
crap anymore, can't read a menu without
glasses, her night vision awful. *Damn air-
lines. Damn delays and cancellations.* The
only rental car left, one with four cylinders,
got the pep of a sea cow.

"I'm trying to reach Detective Jones," she
tells the man who answers the phone.

"Been quite awhile since I was called
that," the voice pleasantly says. "And who's
this?"

She introduces herself, says, "As I understand it, sir, you were a detective with the
Asheville PD back in the eighties, and I'm
wondering if you might remember another
detective named Mark Holland."

"Not well because he'd only been a detective a couple of months when he got
killed."

"What do you remember about that?"

"Only he'd gone to Charlotte supposedly
to interview some witness in a robbery
case. You want to know my opinion, he
wasn't no accident. I think he just didn't
want to take his own life in a place where
one of us would have had to work his case."

"You have any idea why he might have wanted to take his own life?"

"The way I heard it, his wife was cheating on him," he says.

Nana is asleep on the couch, in her long, black robe, her long, white hair loose and splayed over the cushion, Clint Eastwood on the TV, making somebody's day with his big, bad gun.

Win sets down Miss Dog and she instantly puts her head in Nana's lap. Animals always react to her like that. She opens her eyes, looks at Win, holds out her hands to him.

"My darling." She kisses his face.

"You didn't have your alarm on again. So I have no choice but to give you a guard dog. This is Miss Dog."

"Welcome my friend Miss Dog." She pets her, gently pulls on her ears. "Don't you worry, Miss Dog. She won't find you here. That nasty woman, I can see her plain as day, could use a few teeth, couldn't she." Petting Miss Dog. "Don't you worry, my little one," Nana says indignantly. "I have ways of taking care of people like her."

If you want to incur Nana's wrath, treat an animal badly, incite her to go out on one of her mysterious missions late at night, flinging 999 pennies into a bad person's yard, a payment to the old crone goddess Hecate, who knows how to take care of cruel people.

Miss Dog is fast asleep in Nana's lap.

"Her hips are hurting," she says. "Arthritis. Gum problems, pain. Depressed. She yells at her a lot, that big, unhappy woman, not a nice person, treats her the same way she treats herself. Terrible. Poor baby." Petting her as she snores. "I know all about it," she then says to Win. "It's all over TV, but you're all right." She takes his hand. "You remember that time your father beat up that man who lived three streets over?" She points. "He had no choice."

Win isn't sure he knows what she's talking about, nothing new. Her world isn't always obvious or logical.

"You were four and this man's son—he was eight—shoved you to the ground and started kicking you, calling you awful names, calling your father awful names, racist names, and oh, when your father found out, he went to their house and that was that."

"Did Dad start it?"

"Not your father. But he ended it. It happens. And you're all right. If you go back and look around, you'll find a knife."

"No, Nana. It was a gun."

"There's a knife. You know, the kind with a handle that's got a thing." She draws it in the air. Maybe she means a knife with a guard, like a dagger. "You look. The one you killed, and you mustn't blame yourself for that. He was very bad, but there's another one. He's worse. Evil. I tried the honey on a muffin this morning. Tennessee is a pure place with lots of good people, not necessarily good politics, but good people. The bees don't care about politics so they like it there, are joyful making their honey."

Win laughs, gets up. "I think I'm going to head down to North Carolina, Nana."

"Not yet. You have unfinished business here."

"Will you please set the burglar alarm?"

"I have my wind chimes. And Miss Dog," she says. "Tonight the moon is aligned with Venus, has entered Scorpio. Misconceptions abound, my darling. Your perceptions are veiled, but that's all about to change. Go back to her house and you'll find what I'm talking about and something else." She stares off, says, "Why am I seeing a small room with rafters overhead? And a narrow staircase, maybe plywood?"

"Probably because I still haven't gotten around to cleaning out your attic," he says.

11

The next morning Sykes and the director of NFA, Tom, are squatting, moving through the grass like crabs, picking up brass.

On the Knoxville Police Department firing range, no one is above picking up after himself, and everyone is expected to live up to the privilege of attending the Academy. Showing up for class goes without saying. Sykes is sleep-deprived and depressed as she glances around at her classmates, fifteen men and women in blue cargo pants, polo shirts, and caps, returning firearms and ammo to the golf cart, finishing up an eight o'clock session of analyzing trajectories, cartridge case ejections, marking evidence with tiny orange flags and taking photographs like they do at crime scenes.

Sykes is humiliated, dejected, certain the other students are shunning her, have no respect for her. The way it must look to them, she's a fair-weather crime scene investigator, turns up when there's something fun going on like firing the AK-47, the Glock, the 12-gauge riot gun, blasting away at what she calls the *ugly bastard targets,* her favorite because it is far more gratifying to rip into a paper thug pointing a pistol at her than to go for a bull's-eye. She clinks several brass cartridge cases into the plastic bucket she and Tom share, the air humid and heavy, the distant Smoky Mountains hazy, living up to their name.

"So far it's not making the Knoxville PD look good." She is trying to explain, sweat running into her eyes.

"Yesterday was blunt-force and pattern injuries," Tom says, clinking in another cartridge case.

"Kind of funny," she says, parting grass, plucking out more brass. "That's what killed her. Blunt force." Clink. "And she had pattern injuries." Clink. "Win says she had holes punched in her skull, like maybe somebody went after her with a hammer." Clink. "So I'm learning about it anyway, even if I missed class."

"You've missed drug-abuse deaths. SIDS. Child abuse," Tom goes on, moving through the grass, clinking more brass into the bucket.

"You know I'll make it up." She's not sure she can and Win isn't here to help her.

"You've got to." Tom gets to his feet, stretches his back, his young face serious, maybe more serious than he really feels.

He's not the hardhead he pretends to be. Sykes knows. She's seen him with his kids.

"What about the PD, exactly," he then says.

She explains about Jimmy Barber's basement, about a case file that should never have been taken home and now is missing, tells him about what is seeming like an incredibly careless and inept investigation of an incredibly vicious murder. She's a bit dramatic, emphatic, hoping he'll understand the importance of what she's doing instead of focusing on what she's not doing.

"I don't want to make anybody look bad,"

she says. "And if I just drop all this and walk away . . . ? If Win and I do?"

"Don't make excuses for him. He can answer for himself. If we ever see him again. And it's his case, Sykes. His department put him on it."

It may be his case, but that's not how it's feeling. Seems to her she's doing all the work.

"And the KPD isn't going to look bad. That was a long time ago, Sykes. Law enforcement has changed dramatically in the past twenty years. Back then all they had was ID techs, nothing like this." He looks around at his students.

"Well, I don't think I can turn my back on it and walk away," she says.

"Our Academy students don't turn their backs and walk away from anything," Tom says, almost kindly. "Tell you what. Tomorrow's gunshot wounds, we'll be working with a couple ballistic gelatin dummies."

"Well, hell." She likes shooting up jelly men, as she calls them, even more than the ugly bastard targets.

"Not as crucial as some other things, I can let it slide, find some time later to get you back out on the range. But all next week is bloodstain-pattern analysis. That you can't miss."

She takes off her dark blue cap, wipes the sweat off her brow, watches the other students walking off toward the field house, toward the trucks, toward their futures.

"I'll give you until Monday," he says.

"Nothing," Win announces as he creaks down the creaking wooden stairs, remembering how loud they sounded only a few early mornings ago, when his entire life changed.

"I told you. We really did play detective and look around after the fact," Sammy says from a wing chair near a fireplace covered with a stained-glass screen. "No other areas of the house were involved. It fits with what she said. He came in behind her, forced her up to the bedroom, and that was it, thanks to you."

"That wasn't it, unfortunately." Win looks around.

Lamont's glass fetish doesn't end in her office. Win has never seen anything quite like it. Every light fixture is the same kind he shattered in her bedroom, an exotic half moon suspended from a hammered iron chain, hand-painted in vivid colors, signed Ulla Darni, expensive as hell. Her dining-room table is glass, and there are crystal bowls and figurines, art glass mirrors and vases everywhere.

"You know what I'm saying." Sammy gets up slowly, sighs, as if he's too tired to move. "Man oh man. I need a new back. You satisfied? Can we go now?"

"She's got a garage," Win reminds him.

"Already been in there. Nothing."

"I haven't been in there."

"Whatever you want," Sammy says, shrugging, and out the door they go.

In the late eighteen-hundreds, it was a carriage house, brick, a slate roof, now a bit tired and half hidden by the low branches of an old oak tree. Sammy finds the key to the side door, realizes the lock is broken, has been pried open.

"It wasn't like this when I was here. . . ." Sammy slides out his gun. Win's already got his out.

Sammy shoves the door open and it bangs against the inside wall, and he lowers his pistol, returns it to its holster. Win lowers his .357, stands just inside the door, looking around, noticing oil stains on concrete, noticing dirty tire tracks, what he would expect inside a garage. Hanging from Peg-Boards are the usual yard and garden tools, and in a corner is a lawn mower, a wheelbarrow, and a plastic gallon gas can, half full.

"Doesn't look like the gas can came from in here," Sammy remarks.

"Never thought it did," Win replies. "You plan on torching a place, usually you bring your own accelerants."

"Unless it's an inside job, like a domestic situation. Seen my share of those."

"That's not what this is. Roger Baptista sure as hell wasn't a domestic situation," Win says, looking at a rope hanging from the exposed beam ceiling, a pull-down ladder.

"You already check?" Win asks.

Sammy looks up where Win is looking and says, "No."

The windows of the imposing Tudor home glint in the sun, the Tennessee River bright blue and gracefully bending in either direction as far as Sykes can see. She climbs out of her old VW Rabbit, figures she looks like a harmless, middle-aged Realtor in a denim pants suit.

The businessman who owns the house where Vivian Finlay was murdered isn't in, Sykes checked, wonders if anyone has bothered to tell him that twenty years ago a seventy-three-year-old woman was beaten to death inside his ritzy house. If he was told, he must not care. That's something. Sykes wouldn't live in a place where someone was murdered, not even if it was given to her. She starts walking around, wondering how Mrs. Finlay's killer got in.

There's the front door, and on both sides of the house plenty of windows, but they're small, and it's hard for her to imagine someone climbing through a window in the middle of this neighborhood in the middle of the day. Another door closer to the back of the house appears to lead into the basement, then facing the river is one more door, and through windows on either side of it is a handsome modern kitchen with stainless-steel appliances and lots of tiles and granite.

Sykes stands in the backyard, taking in the flowers and lush trees, the low wall built of river rock, then the dock and the water. She watches a motorboat roaring past, pulling a hotdog skier, calls a number she stored in her cell phone as she was driving over here after an Academy class that might be the last one she ever attends.

"Sequoyah Hills Country Club," a polite voice answers.

"The business office, please," Sykes says, and the call is transferred, then, "Missy? Hi. Special Agent Delma Sykes again."

"Well, I can tell you this much," Missy says. "Vivian Finlay was a member from April 1972 until October 1985 . . ."

"October? She died in August," Sykes interrupts.

"October was probably when her family got around to canceling her membership. These things can take awhile, you know, people don't even think about it."

Sykes feels stupid. What does she know about country clubs or memberships of any type?

"Had a full membership," Missy is explaining, "meaning it included tennis and golf."

"What else you got in that file?" Sykes asks, sitting on the wall, wishing she could look at water without trespassing or going on vacation. Must be something to have so much money you can help yourself to a river.

"I'm sorry?"

"I mean, old itemized bills that might give some details as to what she bought and did, maybe? For instance, if she ever bought tennis clothes in the pro shop?"

"We don't throw away business files, but they wouldn't be here in the office. We have a storage facility. . . ."

"I need her old bills, all of them for 'eighty-five."

"My word, twenty years' worth to dig through. That could take . . ." Dismay, an audible sigh.

"I'll help you look," Sykes says.

The upper story of Lamont's garage has been converted into a guest room that doesn't appear to have been used except for the indentations and a little dirt left by feet walking around the dark brown carpet. Fairly big feet, Win notes. Two different tread patterns.

The walls are painted beige and hung

with several signed prints—sailboats, sea-scapes. There is a single bed covered with a brown spread, a bedside table, a small dresser, a swivel chair, and a desk that has nothing on it except an ink blotter, a green glass lamp, and a brass letter opener that looks like a dagger. The furniture is inexpensive maple. A small bathroom with a stacked washer-dryer, very neat and clean, looks unlived-in, except, of course, for the footwear indentations all over the carpet.

"What you got up there?" Sammy yells from the bottom of the pull-down plywood stairs. "Want me to come up?"

"No need and there's no room," Win says, looking down through the opening at the top of Sammy's graying head. "Doesn't look like anybody's been staying here, working here. Or if they were, they moved out and cleaned up pretty well. For sure, someone or maybe more than one person has been walking around."

Win pulls a pair of latex gloves out of a pocket, puts them on, starts opening drawers, all of them. He gets down on his hands and knees, looks under the dresser, looks under the bed, something telling him to look everywhere, not sure what for or why except that if someone has been in and out of the apartment, obviously since it was cleaned and vacuumed last, then why? And who pried open the locked door downstairs? Did someone come here after Lamont was almost murdered, and if so, what was the person looking for? He opens a closet, opens cabinets under the sinks in the kitchenette and the bathroom, stands in the middle of the living room, looks around some more, his attention wandering to the oven. He walks to it and opens the door.

On the bottom rack is a thick manila envelope with the handwritten address of the DA's office and a Knoxville return address, lots of stamps pasted on crooked, hastily, more postage than needed.

"Jesus Christ," he says.

The envelope has been slit open, and he looks at the letter opener on the desk, the one that reminds him of a dagger. He pulls out a thick case file bound with rubber bands.

"You're shittin' me!" he exclaims.

Sammy's feet sound on the pull-down stairs.

"The case. She's had it here all along." Then he's not so sure. "Or someone has."

"Huh?" Sammy's baffled face appears in the opening.

"The Finlay case file."

Sammy holds on to a rope railing, doesn't climb up any farther, says, "Huh?" again.

Win holds up the file, says, "She's had it for three damn months. Since before I started the Academy, before she'd even told me I was going. Christ."

"That doesn't make sense. If Knoxville PD sent it to her, wouldn't they have mentioned that when you started looking for it?"

"No name." Win is reading the label again. "Just the address, which I don't recognize. Postmark June tenth. Zip code's 37921, the Western Avenue–Middlebrook Pike area. Hold on."

He calls Sykes, gets his answer, goes calm the way he does when everything is unraveling. The return address is Jimmy Barber's.

"Looks like his Roller Derby wife dug in the basement long before you did," Win says to Sykes. "Sent the Finlay file up here where it's been hiding in an oven."

"A what? The bitch lied to me!"

"That depends. Did you ever tell her exactly what you were looking for?" Win asks.

Silence.

"Sykes? You there? Did you tell her?"

"Well, not exactly," she says.

At half past two, he parks Nana's old Buick behind her house, can see her wind chimes in daylight, their long, hollow tubes moving in the trees and from the eaves and not quite as magical as they are at night.

Another car is parked near the basketball hoop, almost in the bushes, an old red Miata. He needs a landline and right now his apartment seems like a bad idea. He has a feeling about it and has decided to heed it, wouldn't be far-fetched to suppose cops or someone who pries open locks might be patrolling his neighborhood. He knocks, then walks in through the back door, into the kitchen, where Nana sits across from a distraught young woman who is cutting the deck of tarot cards into three stacks. Nana has made hot tea, a house specialty, with sticks of cinnamon and fresh slivers of lemon peel. He notices a jar of Tennessee honey on the counter, a spoon nearby.

"Guess what we tried, my darling," Nana says to him, reaching for a card. "Your special honey made by joyful bees. This is Suzy. We're taking care of that husband of hers who thinks he doesn't have to abide by the restraining order."

"He been arrested?" Win asks Suzy, in her twenties, delicate-looking, face puffy from crying.

"My boy's a detective," Nana proudly says, sipping her tea as nails click and Miss Dog wanders in.

Win sits on the floor, starts petting her, and she wants her tummy scratched, and Suzy is saying, "Twice. Don't do any good. Matt just bails himself out, shows up like last night at my mama's house, waiting behind the hedge, and gets in my face as I'm getting out of the car. He'll kill me. I know it. People don't understand."

"We'll see about that," Nana warns.

Win asks her where her mama lives, notices Miss Dog is looking remarkably improved. Her sightless eyes seem full of light. She seems to be smiling.

"Just down the road," Suzy tells him with a question in her voice. "You should know." She looks at Miss Dog.

He gets it. Suzy's mother is Miss Dog's

owner. That figures. "Miss Dog's not going anywhere," he says, and that's that.

"I don't care, won't say a word. Mama's awful to her. Matt's worse. I've been telling her the same thing you have. She's gonna get run over by a car."

"Miss Dog's doing just fine," Nana says. "She slept in my bed last night with both the cats."

"So Mama doesn't protect you from Matt." Win gets off the floor.

"Nothing she can do. He cruises past her house all he wants. Walks right in if he wants. She doesn't do anything."

Win heads into the living room to use the phone. He sits among his grandmother's crystals and mystical clutter and asks to speak to Dr. Reid, a geneticist who works for the DNA lab in California that is analyzing the bloody clothing in the Finlay case. He's told Dr. Reid is on a conference call, can get back with Win in half an hour, and he walks out of the house, starts walking toward Miss Dog's house, her former house. He's seen Matt before, pretty sure of it, small, fat, lots of tattoos, the type to be an abusive bully.

His cell phone rings. Sykes.

"Don't bother me. I'm about to get into a fight," he says.

"I'll make this quick, then."

"No sense of humor today?"

"Well, I didn't want to tell you. But if you and me aren't back in class by Monday, we're getting kicked out of the Academy."

It will disappoint her more than it will disappoint him. The Massachusetts State Police has its own crime scene investigators, doesn't need Win out there gathering evidence himself, and he doesn't give a damn about being director of the crime labs or anything else at the moment. It enters his mind that maybe he's lost his enthusiasm because he suspects the only reason he was sent down South to school was to set him up to work the Finlay case, to position him for selfish, political, and, at this point, unknown purposes. And he's no longer sure who is behind what.

"Win?" Sykes is asking.

The house is in sight, about a block up ahead on the left, a white Chevy truck in the drive.

"Don't worry," Win says. "I'll take care of it."

"You can't take care of it! I'm going to be

in so much trouble with the TBI, probably get fired. I wish you wouldn't keep saying you'll fix something you can't, Win!"

"I told you I'm going to take care of it," he says, walking faster as Matt emerges from the back of the house, heading to the pickup truck, that brazen, stupid loser.

"I should tell you the other thing," Sykes says dejectedly. "I checked with Ms. Trailer-Park Barber. Soused again, by the way. And you were right."

"And?" Win begins to trot.

"She sent the case to the DA's office about two months ago, said some guy, sounded young, kind of rude, called her, gave her instructions. She didn't mention it to me because I didn't ask, says a lot of people call about stuff. I'm sorry."

"Gotta go," Win says, running fast.

He grabs the truck's door as it is shutting, and the fat little bully looks at him, shocked, then furious.

"Get your damn hands off my truck!"

He's mean, stupid, stinks like beer and cigarettes, his breath so bad Win can smell it as he opens the door wide, stands between it and the front seat. He looks into the small, cruel eyes of Suzy's worthless husband, who's probably been hanging around here, waiting for her to show up or, if nothing else, waiting for her to drive past and see him and speed off in terror.

"Who are you and what do you want!" Matt yells.

Win just stares at him, a trick he learned a long time ago on the school playground, after he got bigger, got tired of being picked on. The longer you stare at somebody and don't say anything, the more freaked out the person gets, and Matt's eyes seem to be retreating like little clams digging into the sand, hiding. He's not so tough now. Win stands there, blocking the door, staring at him.

"Man, you're crazy," Matt says, beginning to panic.

Silence.

"Now just go on, I'm not doing nothing to nobody." He's spitting as he talks, so scared he just might soil himself.

Silence.

Then Win says, "I hear you're into kicking dogs and abusing your wife."

"That's a lie!"

Silence.

"Whoever said that's lying!"

Silence.

Then, "I just want you to remember my face," Win says very quietly, staring, not a trace of emotion. "You bother Suzy one more time, ever hurt an animal one more time, and this face is going to be the last one you ever see."

Win gets the frustrating news that the DNA analysis isn't completed yet. He explains that the situation is urgent, asks how quickly the analysis can be finished. Maybe in another day or so. He asks exactly what the results might mean.

"A genealogical history," Dr. Reid explains over the phone. "Based on four major bio-geographical ancestry groups, sub-Saharan African, Indo-European, East Asian, or Native American, or an admixture."

Win sits in Nana's favorite rocking chair by the open window, and wind chimes quietly chime, light, sweetly.

". . . Technology based on SNPs," Dr. Reid is explaining. "Single Nucleotide Polymorphisms. Different from normal DNA screening that requires the analysis of millions of base pairs of genes when looking for patterns, many of them irrelevant. Basically, what we're interested in are the some two thousand ancestry information markers. . . ."

Win listens to a typical scientist typically overexplaining, going on and on about some beta version of some machine that is 99.99 percent accurate, about some test that can predict human eye color from DNA with 95 percent accuracy, about Harvard Medical School and a license the lab has with it to develop some anemia drug . . .

"Whoa." Win stops rocking. "What do drugs have to do with this?"

"Pharmacogenetics. When we started doing ancestral profiling, it wasn't to work criminal cases. The original objective was to assist pharmaceutical companies with determining how genetics can be applied to developing drugs."

"You've got something going on with Harvard Medical School?" Win gets a feeling, a strong one.

"Maybe you've heard of PROHEMOGEN? For the treatment of anemia associated with renal failure, cancer chemotherapy, Zidovudine-treated HIV. Can help reduce the need for blood transfusion."

A breeze stirs the trees beyond Nana's window and the chimes seem to chime louder.

"Dr. Reid," Win says, "you mind telling me how long ago the sample was submitted in the Finlay case."

"I believe about two months or so ago."

"It takes that long?"

"Theoretically, five days, a week, but it's a question of priorities. We're currently analyzing DNA in a hundred or so other active criminal cases, several of them serial rapists, serial murderers. I was told there was no rush."

"I understand. Twenty years ago. The guy we're talking about probably isn't killing people anymore."

"It's not a guy. The first thing we always do is run a standard STR panel, which happens to give us gender from one of those markers. Both DNA sources are from females."

"Both? What?"

"Samples from areas of clothing around

the neck, under the arms, the crotch, where you might find cells from sweat, skin shedding, gave us a profile of a female who has a different DNA profile from the bloodstains, which have always been assumed to be the victim's and are," he says. "That much they got right back then."

The storage facility where the country club keeps decades of records is a massive complex of cinder-block units connected like train cars over a two-acre lot.

Although the units are temperature-controlled, they have no lighting, and Sykes runs the narrow beam of her small flashlight over white cartons while Missy checks her inventory list so she can tell what's inside.

"E-three," Sykes reads.

"November 1985," Missy says. "Getting close."

They move on. It is stuffy in here, dusty, and Sykes is getting tired of digging through old boxes in dark, claustrophobic spaces while Win runs around New England doing who knows what.

"E-eight," she reads.

"June 1985. Looks like they're a bit out of order."

"You know what?" Sykes decides, lifting another heavy box off metal shelving. "Let's just get them for the whole year."

The doorman of the historic brick building in Beacon Hill isn't inclined to let Win do what he wants, which is to appear at Lamont's door unannounced.

"I'm sorry, sir," says the older man in his gray uniform, a bored doorman who spends most of his time behind a desk, obviously reading newspapers. There's a stack of them under his chair. "I have to ring her first. What's your name?"

Numb-nut. You just told me she's home.

"All right. I guess you leave me no choice." Win sighs, reaching inside his jacket pocket, slipping out his wallet, flipping it open, showing his creds. "But I really need you to keep quiet about this. I'm in the middle of an extremely sensitive investigation."

The doorman takes a long time looking at Win's shield, his ID card, then looks closely at his face, something odd and uncertain in his own, maybe a glint of excitement, then,

"You're that . . . ? The one I've been reading about. I recognize you now."

"I can't talk about it," Win says.

"You want my opinion, you did what you had to do. Damn right. Kids these days, worthless hoodlums."

"I can't talk about it," Win says as a woman in her fifties enters the lobby, yellow designer suit, a Chanelian, as Win calls rich women who have to flaunt those huge Chanel double C's.

"Good afternoon." The doorman politely nods at her, almost bows.

She dismisses Win's existence, then does a sharp double take, stares openly at him, smiles at him, a little flirtation going. He smiles back, watches her head to the elevator.

"I'll just ride up with her," Win says to the doorman, doesn't give him a chance to protest.

He strides across the lobby as polished brass elevator doors part and steps aboard a mahogany vessel that is about to carry him on a mission Monique Lamont isn't likely to appreciate or forget.

"They really need to replace this. How many times do I need to tell them? As if the building can't afford a new elevator," the Chanelian says, tapping the button for the eighth floor, looking him over as if he's a trunk show and she might just buy everything in it.

The elevator creaks like the *Titanic* sinking. Lamont is staying in this building but no one seems to know which apartment. There isn't one in her name.

"You live in the building? Don't believe I've seen you before," the Chanelian says.

"Just visiting." He looks confused, staring at the elevator buttons. "She said the penthouse, but there seem to be two of them. PH and PH two. Or maybe it was . . . ?" He starts digging in his pockets, as if looking for notes.

The elevator stops. The doors take their time opening. The Chanelian doesn't move, gets thoughtful, replies, "If you tell me who you're here to see, perhaps I can help you."

He clears his throat, lowers his voice, leans closer, her perfume piercing his sinuses like an ice pick. "Monique Lamont, but please keep that confidential."

Her eyes light up, she nods. "Tenth floor, south corner. But she doesn't live here. Just visits. Often. Probably to have a little privacy. Everyone is entitled to a life." Her eyes on his. "If you know what I mean."

"You know her?" he asks.

"Know of. She's rather hard to miss. And people talk. And you? You look familiar."

Win sticks out his arm, keeps the doors from closing, replies, "A lot of people say that. Have a nice rest of the day."

The Chanelian doesn't like being dismissed, walks off, doesn't look back. Win gets out his cell phone, calls Sammy.

"Do me a favor. Lamont's apartment." He gives Sammy the address. "Find out who owns it, who leases it, whatever."

He gets off on the tenth floor, where there are two doors on either side of a small marble foyer, and he rings the bell for 10 SC. He rings it three times before Lamont's wary voice sounds on the other side.

"Who is it?"

"It's me, Win," he says. "Open the door, Monique."

Locks unlock, the heavy wooden door opens, Lamont on the other side, looking like hell, looking like she just got out of the shower.

"What do you want? You had no right coming here," she says furiously, pushing damp hair out of her face. "How did you get in?"

He moves past her, stands beneath a Baccarat chandelier, looks around at ornate molding and wainscoting and rich, old wood.

"Nice place you've got here. Worth what? A couple mil? Four or five, maybe six?" he says.

Sykes sits inside an office at a club she could never afford and wonders if Vivian Finlay thought she was better than everybody else and would have dismissed Sykes as a klutzy country girl who probably doesn't know which fork to use for salad. The truth about crime victims is, a lot of them are unlikable.

She sorts through paperwork, has gotten as far as May. What she has learned so far is that Mrs. Finlay was very active, played tennis at the country club as often as three times a week, always had lunch afterward, and based on how much the bill was each time, she never ate alone and had a habit of picking up the check. It appears she ate dinner there once or twice a week and liked Sunday brunch. Again, she didn't dine alone, based on the substantial size of the bills.

Mrs. Finlay was conspicuously generous, and Sykes suspects the reason for the rich old woman's largesse wasn't so she could spread around her good fortune, since it is unlikely that her guests were on tight budgets, not at this club. More likely, she was one of those people who nod for the check every time because she likes to be the big shot, likes to be in charge, controlling people, proud people, the sort who have always made Sykes feel simple and small. She's dated plenty of men like that, thinks about how different Win is from any man she's ever known.

Like the other night at the Tennessee Grill, the two of them watching the sun set over the river, a special evening of big cheeseburgers and beer, her aching with the hope that maybe he was as attracted to her as she was to him. Well, *is.* She can't deny it, keeps thinking it will go away. That night it was her turn to treat, and she did because unlike most men, Win doesn't mind—not that he's cheap, because he sure isn't. He's generous and kind but believes things ought to be equal so both people feel *em-*

powered and experience the pleasure of giving, is the way he explains it. Win takes turns. On the firing range, driving places, paying tabs, or just talking, he is as fair as he can be.

Sykes begins looking through the statement for the month of July, starts getting excited when she notices that in addition to Mrs. Finlay's court times and lunches, a *guest* played tennis and golf at the club. Whoever this *guest* was, or perhaps it was a different guest on different occasions, Sykes considers, within a two-week period, almost two thousand dollars was spent on "clothing" in the pro shops and charged to Mrs. Finlay's account. Sykes starts on the month of August.

On the eighth, the day Mrs. Finlay was murdered, a *guest* played tennis, apparently alone because there is a rental fee for the ball machine, something it doesn't seem the sociable Mrs. Finlay ever used. That same day, a *guest* spent almost a thousand dollars in the tennis pro shop and charged it to Mrs. Finlay's account.

———

There is nothing between Lamont and Win except an antique table and her red silk robe.

It is almost seven p.m., the sun fiery orange, a band of pink spreading across the horizon, the window open and warm air drifting in.

"Why don't you get dressed," he says to her for the third time. "Please. We're two professionals, two colleagues talking. Let's keep it like that."

"You're not here because we're colleagues. And it's my apartment and I'll wear what I want."

"Actually, it's not your apartment," he says. "Sammy had a little chat with the supervisor. It seems your crime lab director is doing quite well."

She is silent.

"Monique? Where does Huber get his money?"

"Why don't you ask him."

"Why are you staying in his apartment? The two of you got something going?"

"I'm rather homeless at the moment. Get this over with, won't you?"

"All right. We'll get back to that." Win leans forward, rests his elbows on the table.

"I can go first or give you a chance to tell me the truth."

"Yes, colleagues, as you put it." Her eyes are on his. "Will you Mirandize me next for some crime you seem to think I've committed?"

"Truth." He says it again. "You're in trouble. I can't help you if you don't tell me the truth."

"I have no idea what you're talking about."

"The office over your garage," he goes on. "Who uses it?"

"Did you get a search warrant before you went charging in there?"

"Your property is a crime scene. All of it, every inch of it. I don't need to explain that to you."

She picks up a pack of cigarettes, slides one out, her hands trembling. It's the first time he's ever seen her smoke.

"When's the last time you were in the apartment over your garage?" he asks.

She lights the cigarette, takes a deep drag, is considerate enough to blow smoke out sideways instead of in his face.

"What is it you intend to accuse me of?"

"Come on, Monique. I'm not after you."

"Feels like it." She slides an ashtray close.

"Here, let me walk you through it." Win tries a different approach. "I enter your garage through the side door—which, by the way, had been broken into, the lock pried open."

She blows out smoke, taps an ash, a glint of fear that turns to anger.

"And I see some evidence of a car having been in there, tire tracks, dirty, possibly made when it rained last. Which would have been the night you were attacked."

She listens, smokes.

"I see the pull-down stairs and climb up and find a guest apartment that appears un-lived-in except for footprints on the carpet."

"And of course, you ransacked the place," she says, leaning back in her chair as if invit-ing him to look at her in a way he shouldn't.

"If I did, what did I find? Why don't you tell me?"

"I have no idea," she says.

13

Lamont taps an ash, blowing out smoke, her eyes not leaving his, her robe nothing but a red sheen over her naked flesh, tied tightly around her waist, cleavage showing.

"All these high-tech labs you deal with in California?" Win is saying. "There's a lot of money in biotechnology, pharmaceuticals. A lot of potential for fraud, scams. Funny how stuff like that metastasizes from person to person. Sometimes to people who weren't bad, then got exposed."

She is listening, smoking, looking at him, the same unsettling glint in her eyes.

He exclaims, "Are you hearing me?"

"You going to play bad cop now, Win? Won't work. I know the routine better than you do."

"You think you can do this to me?" he says. "Agree to have me sent off to Tennessee, then jerk me back up here to work this publicity-stunt case of yours. A threatening letter. Accusations that the shooting wasn't a good one, how could you do that to me, what kind of person would do something like that . . . ?"

"A suggestion that the shooting had to be investigated. A suggestion made by a DA who plays by the rules." Her eyes stare at him. "I played it by the books."

"Oh yeah. You and your rules. You and your ego and machinations. A missing police file, a homicide case file no one's been able to find. Well, guess what. I found it. And guess where. In your damn apartment over the garage. Are you crazy?"

"What?" She looks confused, startled.

"You heard me."

"The Finlay case file was in my garage apartment? I didn't even know it was missing or that my office ever had it. . . . Where in my apartment?"

"You tell me." He is getting very angry.

"I would if I knew!"

"How about the oven."

"Is this supposed to be funny?"

"The Vivian Finlay case file was in your oven."

The look returns to her eyes, suspicion, contempt. "Somebody stoned and damn stupid," she mutters. "Someone with the memory of a gnat. To make me look bad."

"You hide it in there?"

"I'm not stupid," she says, crushing out her cigarette as if she's killing it slowly. "Thank you, Win. You've just given me extremely important information."

She leans forward, rests her arms on the table, affording him a view he shouldn't have, her eyes filled with an invitation she has never offered in the past.

"Stop it, Monique," he says.

She doesn't move, waits, watching him look, and his eyes have a will of their own, and it enters his mind more than it ever has before what it would be like with her . . .

"Don't do this." He looks away. "I know what you must feel. I've worked with victims of sexual violence. . . ."

"You don't know anything! I'm not a victim!"

Her outburst seems to shake the kitchen.

"And I'm not going to be one," he says quietly, coldly. "You're not going to use me to validate that you're still desirable. Save it for your therapist."

"*You* validate *me*?" she says, snatching her robe together. "I believe it's the other way around. I believe I would be the one doing the validating." She sits up straight in the chair, looking down, blinking back tears.

A long silence follows as she struggles to control herself.

Then, "I'm sorry." She wipes her eyes. "Unfair and I'm sorry. I didn't mean that."

"Talk to me," Win says.

"If you'd bothered to look into all this a little more thoroughly"—she regains her composure and sharp edge—"you might have found out I don't use the garage. Haven't parked my car in there for months. Someone else does. Or did. I haven't stepped foot inside the place."

"Who?"

"Toby."

"Toby?" he says furiously, feeling something else. "You've been letting that brain-dead idiot live on your property? Jesus."

"You sound jealous." She smiles, smoking.

"And you sound like you think you owe Huber. . . ." His thoughts are tangled. He almost sputters.

"It doesn't matter."

"It does matter!"

"He asked if Toby could live there while clerking for me. Get him out of the house."

Win thinks of the hundred-dollar bills in Baptista's pocket, the gasoline can, the rags. He thinks of the missing keys that forced Lamont to go around to the back of her house, where it was dark and wooded, so she could get the spare key out of the box. He thinks of Toby's penchant for drugs, thinks of Baptista's drug charges and recent visit to juvenile court.

"Let me ask you something," Win says. "You know any reason why Huber might want you dead?"

Lamont lights another cigarette, her voice getting hoarse from smoke. She's laying off the martinis, is pouring herself a glass of white wine.

She watches him, appraises him, watches

him watching her, waiting for his eyes to find her. My God, he is the most beautiful male specimen she has ever seen. Dark, pleated trousers; open-neck white cotton shirt; smooth, tan skin; hair as black as a raven's; and eyes that change like the weather. She reminds herself that she's a little drunk, wonders what it would be like . . . then stops herself from going there.

Win doesn't say a word. She can't tell what he is thinking.

"I know you have no respect for me," she then says, smoking.

"I feel sorry for you," he says.

"Of course." She feels hate rising, squeezing her heart. "You and your kind take it from us and then cast us aside. Turn us into garbage, then treat us like garbage. Save your pity for one of your loser bimbo girlfriends."

"I feel sorry for you because you're empty."

She laughs and her laugh sounds hollow.

Empty. She feels like crying again, doesn't understand what is wrong with her, in control one minute, falling apart the next.

"Looking for something to fill up your vast emptiness, Monique. The best of everything. Power. Fame. More power. Beauty. Any man you want. All of it so fragile, like all of your glass. The slightest trauma or disappointment and everything breaks."

She turns away from him, won't give him her eyes.

"I'm going to ask you again, did you have anything to do with the Finlay case file ending up in your apartment, where Toby was staying?"

"Why!" She blurts out in a trembling voice, looking at him again. "To keep it from you? No. I told you. I've never even seen that file. I assumed it was in Tennessee."

"Then you didn't see it when it arrived at your office? Toby claims he put it on your desk."

"He's a goddamn liar. I didn't even know it was being sent to my office. Obviously he intercepted it."

"So I'm to assume he took it to your garage apartment and hid it. Or misplaced it. Or whatever the hell he did."

"I don't go in there, not since he's been there. It's just a guest room, rarely used."

"Doesn't appear he used it much, either. You never saw him coming or going?"

"I didn't pay any attention."

"Never saw his car?"

"Sometimes heard it, usually very late at night. I stayed out of his business. Frankly, didn't care. Assumed he was out all the time, partying with his druggie friends."

"Maybe a druggie friend named Roger Baptista. By the looks of it, Toby was never planning on coming back to your office or your apartment after his vacation in the Vineyard."

She is thinking, her face tight, angry. Scared.

"Why would Toby remove that file from your office?" Win presses her.

"Forgetful, brain rotted by drugs, no memory left . . ."

"Monique?"

"Because someone asked him to, what do you think! To make me look incompetent, corrupt. You don't have what you need to work the case. Without the file, it's rather impossible, isn't it? If that file was found there, it's terrible for me."

Win just listens.

"Someone told Toby to take it and the

brain-rotted fool did." She is silent for a minute, then, "Stupid, incompetent. Dead or alive. Either way, Crawley gets reelected."

"You think he had something to do with this?"

"How convenient Toby was out of town that night. When you showed up, when it happened, Toby wasn't there. Had just left for the Vineyard. No witnesses. The purpose of that ridiculous letter left at the Diesel Café was probably to make sure you didn't decide to show up at my house and prevent the very thing you did."

"So you know about that, too," Win says. "Let me guess. Huber and his silk cravats. A scarlet one that night."

"I found out after the fact. Now maybe I see a different reason why he did it. A taunting letter to keep you occupied. In case you might have decided to drop by, come see me . . ."

"Why would he think that?"

"Pathological jealousy. He thinks everybody wants me. He thinks everybody wants you. Toby probably hand-picked him, you're probably right." She's back to something else, back to Baptista. "Probably one of his drug sources. Probably met him hanging around the courthouse. Do you think he paid him?"

"Who's *he*?"

She looks at him, looks at him a long time, then, "You know damn well."

"Huber," Win says, and it's not going to be easy interrogating him when that time comes.

"Jessie's probably the one who broke into my apartment. . . ."

"Why? To find the file?"

"Yes." Then, "I don't know. I don't know. All I know is he wanted me to look bad. Destroy my reputation. After death. Or now. In life . . ."

Her voice is shaking, her eyes filled with enraged tears. Win watches her, waits.

"So tell me." She can barely talk. "He pay him to rape me, too?" She raises her voice, tears falling.

Win doesn't know. He doesn't know what to say.

"Or paid him just to kill me and burn up the house and the worthless nothing piece of shit threw in the rape free. Oh yes. The proverbial crime of opportunity."

"Why?" Win quietly asks. "Why the—"

"Why the *overkill*?" Lamont interrupts

with a harsh laugh. "Why? Come on, Win. You see it every day. Hate. Envy. Being scorned, dissed, threatened. Payback. Kill somebody as many times and in as many different horrific ways as you can, right? Degrade them, cause them as much pain and suffering as possible."

Images of that night, of her. Win tries to push them back.

"Well, he tried," she says. Then, "How much?"

He knows what she's asking. He doesn't answer her.

"How much!"

He hesitates, says, "A thousand dollars."

"So that's all I'm worth."

"It has nothing to do with that and you know—"

"Don't bother," she says.

14

Rex's Guns & Ammo is on Upward Road in East Flat Rock, a good spot for a private meeting because the shop is closed on Sundays. Nice to know that the folks in North Carolina who believe in firearms and camouflage observe the Sabbath.

Sykes and Win sit in folding chairs somewhere between racks of rifles and fishing tackle, a seven-pound bass mounted on the wall giving Sykes the fisheye. Leaning against a glass showcase of pistols is the Henderson County Sheriff, Rutherford, a friend of Rex's, which is how he came upon the key to let Win and Sykes in so they could have a little discussion about the Finlay case. Rutherford sort of looks like his name, an odd thing about that, a phenomenon Sykes has been aware of all her life.

He's big and rumbling like a freight train, intimidating and hell-bent in one direction— his. He has reminded them more than once in one way or another that Flat Rock is his jurisdiction, made it clear that if anybody picks up George and Kimberly, "Kim," Finlay, it will be him, says he needs to understand why they should be picked up in the first place. So Sykes and Win are doing their best to patiently explain the facts of the case, details that became apparent when they stayed up all last night driving here from Knoxville, then holing up in a Best Western Motel, picking apart and piecing together information from a case file that they should have had access to from the start, pages and pages of reports, witness statements, and about a dozen gruesome photographs that make many things disturbingly obvious.

It was Kim who discovered Mrs. Finlay's brutalized body and called 911 at 2:14 p.m., August 8. She claims she was driving George's white Mercedes sedan, was out running errands and decided to drop by for a visit. Yet several hours earlier, between ten thirty and eleven a.m., a retired man who lived only a few blocks from Mrs. Finlay's Sequoyah Hills home saw Kim in the area driving her red Mercedes convertible. When Detective Barber questioned her about it she offered the simple explanation that while she was out and about she stopped in the Sequoyah Hills neighborhood to walk her Maltese, Zsa Zsa, on Cherokee Boulevard, or *the Boulevard,* as she called it. Nothing particularly suspicious about that, since Cherokee Boulevard was and is a popular place for people, including nonresidents, to walk their dogs. Kim, who didn't live in Sequoyah Hills, was known to walk Zsa Zsa there daily, depending on the weather, and August 8 happened to be a beautiful day.

In her statement to Barber, she continued to spin her reasonably credible story, claiming she took Zsa Zsa home around noon, checked on George, who was *sick in bed with a cold,* then went back out in his Mercedes because her Mercedes convertible *needed gas and was making a funny noise.* On her way to the dry cleaner's, she decided to *drop in* on Mrs. Finlay, and when she didn't answer the door Kim let herself in and had *the most awful shock* of her life. She went on to tell Barber, very tearfully, that she had been very worried about Mrs. Finlay's safety. *She has all this money and is ostentatious and lives alone, and is naïve, much too trusting,* she said, adding that earlier in the week when *George and I came by to have dinner with her, we both saw a suspicious-looking black man near her house, staring at it. When we turned into the driveway, he walked away very quickly.*

George, of course, verified his wife's story. George, of course, had a few good stories of his own, including that he was *fairly sure* his aunt had noticed this same black man several days earlier, just walking up and down the street near her house—*loitering,* in her words. George was also *fairly sure* he *probably* left a hammer on a windowsill in his aunt's master bedroom, having used it to help her hang a painting, he wasn't ex-actly sure when, but not long before *it hap-pened.* A plausible theory evolved: Mrs. Fin-lay returned home from tennis or shopping or something and interrupted her assailant, who had gotten only so far as stealing a box of silver coins that supposedly was *in plain view on a dresser in the master bedroom.*

In one of Barber's notes, he wrote that when the police arrived, there was water in the tub, a damp towel draped over the side of it, and another, larger damp towel on the bedroom floor not far from where the body was found. He speculated that when the killer heard Mrs. Finlay drive up, he *may have hid himself* and watched her undress to take a bath, which *may have sexually excited him.* At the point when she may have had nothing on but her *ruffled blue tennis panties,* he confronted her, and when she started screaming, he noticed the hammer on the windowsill and used it.

What Barber didn't entertain, at least not in writing, was the possibility that Mrs. Finlay was in the tub when her assailant appeared, that in fact her assailant might have been someone she knew so well as to allow this person to come into the bedroom, perhaps even talk to her while she was still in the tub or drying off, maybe a close female friend or relative, maybe someone who didn't always get along with her. It never seemed to occur to Barber that Mrs. Finlay might have been murdered by someone very close to her, the crime then staged to look like an attempted sexual assault that went as far as her tennis panties being pulled down to her knees before her enraged assailant beat her to death.

According to the statement of one of Mrs. Finlay's tennis partners, Kim and Mrs. Finlay had gotten quite hostile toward each other over the summer, and Mrs. Finlay *had begun saying things like Chinese people should work in Laundromats, not marry people like her nephew.* Sykes sure as hell would have been on high alert if she had been the detective and someone had told her that, would have zeroed in on all of it, would have connected the dots, decided Kim and Mrs. Finlay pretty much hated each other and maybe when Kim dropped by the house after tennis that day—after yet another shopping spree charged to Mrs. Finlay's country club account—they got into an argument that went no place good.

"Still sounds mighty circumstantial to me," Rutherford the sheriff says from beside the showcase of pistols that is propping him up.

"The DNA isn't circumstantial," Win replies, and he keeps looking at Sykes, as if to remind the sheriff that the two of them are in this together.

"Don't understand why they didn't get the DNA back then. You sure something didn't get contaminated after twenty years?"

"They didn't do DNA testing back then," Win says, looking at Sykes, and she nods. "Just standard serology, ABO typing, which certainly indicated that the blood on the tennis clothing was Mrs. Finlay's. But what they didn't test twenty years ago were areas of clothing that might yield other biological information."

"Like what areas?" the sheriff asks, getting an impatient look on his face.

"Areas that rub against your skin, areas that might have sweat or saliva, other body fluids. Get it from all sorts of things. The inside of collars, under the arms, the brims of hats, socks, the inside of shoes, chewing gum, cigarette butts. We need highly sensitive DNA technology for tests like that. PCR. STR. And by the way, when DNA is contaminated, you don't get false positives."

Rutherford doesn't want to get into it, says, "Well, George and Kim aren't going to give you any trouble. And like I told you, I know they're home. Had my secretary call them up, pretend she was collecting money for the FOP hurricane fund. You ever seen anything like all these hurricanes? The Lord Almighty's unhappy with something, you ask me."

"Plenty to be unhappy about," Sykes says to him. "Plenty of ambition, greed, and hatred, the very same things that led to Mrs. Finlay's murder."

Sheriff Rutherford says nothing, won't look at her, has been addressing his every comment to Win. It's a man's world, probably explaining why there's all these hurricanes, punishment for women not staying home and doing what they're told.

"Before y'all head out," the sheriff says to Win, "I'd like to clear up the train part, because I'm still suspicious it was a homicide, like maybe there was some sort of organized crime involved, Dixie Mafia or something. And if that's so"—he slowly shakes his jowly head—"then maybe we should be approaching this different, bring in the FBI."

"No way it was a homicide." Sykes is adamant. "Everything I've found out about Mark Holland's case indicates suicide."

"And what's everything?" the sheriff asks Win, as if it's Win who just made that claim.

"Like the fact that when he was married to Kim, she went through his money and was cheating on him, having an affair with Mark's best friend, another cop. Mark had plenty of reason to be depressed and angry," she says, looking right at the sheriff.

"Might not have been enough for Barber to run with," Win adds, "but it should have caused him to ask a few questions about Kim's character and morals. Which he clearly did, since he contacted the medical examiner's office in Chapel Hill, then stapled a Polaroid photograph of Holland's remains to the personal-effects inventory from Mrs. Finlay's autopsy."

"A personal-effects inventory that had tennis clothes on it? Because the tennis clothes were size six, he made some Sherlock leap to a train fatality?" Rutherford peels open a stick of spearmint gum, winks at Win, says, "Guess I'll leave my DNA on it, huh?" Then, "Go on." Chewing. "Go on, then. I'm listening. Hook that up with the train fatality. Hope you can." Chewing.

"Ten," Sykes says. "The tennis clothes were size ten."

"Well, not that I'm an expert on women's attire, but I can't see any connection between this poor cop being run over by a train and this dead old lady's tennis clothes. You implying Detective Barber figured those clothes were too big to fit Mrs. Finlay?" He says all this to Win.

"I bet Barber didn't notice," Sykes says.

"Don't think I would have," the sheriff says to Win. "How 'bout you?" He winks at him again, chewing.

"Detective Garano's the one who *did* notice," Sykes says.

"Possibly a simpler answer is the bloody tennis clothes were what Barber submitted to the TBI labs for testing," Win suggests. "He had a copy of it, stapled it to the morgue photo. Tucked them inside his September MasterCard bill, maybe because that's where the previous month's charges were listed for his trip to the ME's office in Chapel Hill. People do things, don't think about them. Who knows."

"That sure is the truth," Sykes agrees, thinking of the case file Toby Huber stupidly stuck in the oven.

"A lot of details never make sense," Win goes on. "A lot of holes never get filled in. A lot of what is reconstructed probably looks very little like what really happens in those minutes, those split seconds, when a violent outburst ends someone's life."

"You some kind of philosopher or something?" Rutherford narrows his eyes, chews his gum.

Win gets up from his chair, looks at Sykes, gives her the signal.

"We just need a little time to give them the happy news, then you can pick them up," Win says to the sheriff.

At least he said "we," Sykes thinks. He didn't have to include her. *It's his case,* she thinks, but no matter how often she reminds herself of that, she feels disappointed, depressed about it, resentful. After all those dark places and boxes and phone calls and missed Academy classes and everything else, it certainly feels like her case, and it would feel pretty damn good to tell Kim and George Finlay they didn't get away with it, that they're about to find themselves in handcuffs and end up in a very different Big House from what they're used to—this one with razor wire.

"They're nice enough folks," Rutherford says to Win as they walk out to the parking lot, takes a good, long, disparaging look at Sykes's old VW Rabbit, same thing he did when she and Win first drove up. "Well, call me when you're ready," he says to Win. "A real shame locking them up." Chewing gum. "They've never caused any trouble around here."

"Doesn't look like they're going to get a chance to, either," Sykes says.

A few miles away is Little River Road, where many of Flat Rock's wealthy residents have big homes and estates, many of them summer homes, many of their owners from the far reaches of New York, Los Angeles, Boston, and Chicago.

Sykes pulls her car off the long, unpaved driveway, parks to one side, in the weeds so she and Win can show up with no advance warning. They get out and start walking toward the house that Vivian Finlay's nephew, George, and his *93 percent East Asian* wife, Kim, inherited from Mrs. Finlay after her murder. The well-off couple have been married twenty-two years, their wedding six months after Kim's first husband, Detective Mark Holland, committed suicide on lonely train tracks in a lonely part of North Carolina.

"Well, I know I would have," Sykes remarks, carrying on a conversation they've been having for the past ten minutes.

"It's easy to say twenty years after the fact," Win reminds her. "We weren't there."

"You mean you wouldn't have bothered checking out the tennis reservations?" Sykes says as they walk along the unpaved drive, getting closer to the house where George and Kim enjoy their privileged lives in their lovely home. "You know, just done the same damn thing I did?"

She has to remind Win yet again of how hard she's worked, of what an amazingly thorough and smart investigation she's conducted.

"If Barber had done that, he would have realized it wasn't Mrs. Finlay who used the ball machine that day," Sykes goes on, has made this point maybe four times now, "not unless she signed in as a *guest.* All he had to do was ask questions."

"Maybe he felt about it a little bit the same way I do," Win suggests. "He didn't like dealing with a club that would never have him as a member."

She walks close to him. He puts his arm around her.

"So, she's going to jail?" Sykes asks, and she isn't talking about Kim Finlay.

She's thinking of Monique Lamont.

"Personally, I think she's been punished plenty," Win says. "But I'm not finished yet."

For a moment they are quiet as they walk in the sun, the driveway long and winding, trees everywhere. He can feel the heaviness in Sykes's heart, sense her pain and disappointment.

"Yeah, you've got a lot of unfinished business up there, all right," she says. "Guess you'll be leaving after you take care of these two." She stares in the direction of the house.

"We could use a few good CSIs in Massachusetts," he says.

She walks with her arm around him, holding him tight.

"You think the box of silver coins ever existed?" she asks, maybe just to change the subject, maybe to get her mind off where Win lives and works, off where he has his life, off how entwined his life is with Lamont's, no matter how much he denies it.

"Probably," he says. "I'm guessing Kim grabbed it on her way out the first time, after she killed her, trying to figure out how to stage it to look like a burglary/sex crime, disguise what in truth was probably an impulse crime. Blame it on a suspicious-looking black man. Worked like a charm, especially back then. People used to call the police on my dad. Happened a lot. He's in his own yard and gets reported as a prowler."

The sun is hot on their heads, the air cool, the roof of the house visible now, peeking above trees. They remove their arms from each other, walking apart, like colleagues again, talking about the case, Sykes wondering why Jimmy Barber never questioned what happened to Vivian Finlay's shoes and socks, wondering what Kim found to wear when she made her getaway after stripping off her bloody tennis clothes, wondering a lot of things.

Then the house is right there in front of them, George and Kim Finlay, now in their sixties, sitting in white chairs on the wide white porch, eating lunch.

Win and Sykes stare at the couple on the porch staring at them.

"They're all yours," he quietly says.

Sykes looks at him. "You sure?"

"It's your case, partner."

They follow the slate walkway, head to the

wooden steps that lead up to the porch, where George and Kim have stopped eating. Then Kim gets up from her chair, a stooped woman with graying hair pinned back, dark-tinted glasses, wrinkles that indicate she scowls a lot.

"Are you lost?" she loudly asks.

"No, ma'am, we're definitely not lost," Sykes says, she and Win stepping onto the porch. "I'm Special Agent Delma Sykes with the Tennessee Bureau of Investigation. This is Investigator Winston Garano, Massachusetts State Police. I talked to you on the phone the other day?" she says to George.

"Why, yes." George clears his throat, a small man, white hair, looks uncertain, pulls his napkin out of the front of his Izod shirt, doesn't seem sure whether he should stand or sit.

"The murder of Vivian Finlay has been reopened due to new evidence," Sykes says.

"What evidence could there possibly be after all these years?" Kim says, acts clueless, even tries to look distressed by the memory.

"Your DNA, ma'am," Sykes says.

15

He and Nana, and a secret mission, mid-October, the night starting out crisp and cool with not much of a moon.

Watertown, driving fast to an address where a client of hers said that dogfights were secretly being held in the basement on the weekends, horrible, violent fights, pugs, terriers, bulldogs, pit bulls, starved, baited, torn to pieces. Twenty dollars, the price of admission.

Win can still see the look on Nana's face as she pounded on the door, see the look on the man's face when she walked right into his dark, squalid house.

I have you between my fingers, she said, holding up two fingers, pinching them together. *And I'm squeezing. Where are the dogs? Because we're taking every one of them right now.* And she squeezed her fingers together as tightly as she could, right in his mean, soulless face.

Crazy witch! He yelled at her.

Go take a look in your yard, look at all those shiny new pennies everywhere, she said, and maybe time has embellished history, but as Win recalls it, the moment she mentioned the pennies and the man went to the window to look, a fierce wind kicked up from nowhere and a tree branch slammed against that very window and shattered it.

Nana and Win drove off with a carload of dogs—pitiful, mangled creatures—while he cried uncontrollably, tried to pet them, do something to make them not hurt and shake so much, and after they left them at the animal hospital, they drove home and it had gotten very cold, and the heat had been turned on inside the house, and Win's mother and father and Pencil were dead.

"Pencil?" Monique Lamont asks from her glass desk.

"A goofy mixed breed yellow Lab, Pencil.

Because as a puppy he was always chewing up my pencils," Win replies.

"CO poisoning."

"Yes."

"That's awful." It sounds so empty when Lamont says it.

"I felt it was my fault," he tells her. "Maybe the same way you feel about what happened to you, that it's somehow your fault. Victims of rape often feel that. And you know that. You've seen it enough in your office, in court."

"I'm not a victim."

"You were raped. You were almost murdered. But you're right. You're not a victim. You were one."

"As were you."

"In a different way, but true."

"How old?" she asks.

"Seven."

"Geronimo," she says. "I've always wondered why *Geronimo*. Courage? Determination? Revenge for the deaths of his family? *The great Apache warrior.*"

She is her old self in a handsome black suit, sunlight lighting up every piece of glass in her office. Win feels as if he's in the middle of a rainbow, a rainbow that is hers. If she tells the truth, the whole truth, there is hope.

"Because you had to become the hero?" she is asking, trying to show warmth and hide her fear. "You had to become the warrior because you were the only one left?"

"Because I felt useless," he says. "Didn't want to do sports, compete, be on teams, do much of anything that might somehow measure me and show how useless I really was. So I kind of kept to myself, reading, drawing, writing, all sorts of solitary things. Nana started calling me Geronimo."

"Because you felt useless?" Lamont reaches for her sparkling water, a blank expression on her striking face.

Nana always reminded him, *You're Geronimo, my darling. Don't ever forget, my darling.*

And Win is saying to Lamont, "One of the many things Geronimo said is, *I cannot think that we are useless or God would not have created us. And the sun, the darkness, the winds are all listening to what we have to say.* So there you have it, what I have to say about myself. The truth, Monique." He adds, "Now it's your turn. I'm here to listen, but only if you plan on telling me every-thing."

She sips water, looks at him, deliberating, then, "Why would you give a damn, Win? Why really?"

"Fairness. The worst things that have happened aren't your fault."

"You'd really care if I went to prison?"

"You don't belong in prison. It wouldn't be fair to the other inmates."

Surprised, she laughs. But her mirth fades quickly. She drinks more water, her hands nervous.

Win says, "This isn't just about your run-ning for governor, is it?"

"Apparently not," she says, keeping her eyes on him. "No, of course not. It was a twofold plan. My losing the Finlay homicide file and then its showing up on my property would have turned At Risk into a farce, turned me and my office into one, ingratiated Huber with the governor, the two of them in on that one together, I have no doubt. Either I'm murdered or I'm ruined or both, really. No one saying nice things at my funeral. Use-less. I know that word, too, Geronimo." She pauses, looking at him. "Useless and fool-ish."

"The governor want you murdered?"

She shakes her head. "No. He just didn't want me to win the election. Jessie wanted the governor to be grateful to him—how the hell do you think he's gotten where he is in life? Favors. Manipulations. He wanted me dead and, oh well, that certainly would have made life easier for Crawley, too, but no. Our dear governor wouldn't have the stomach for that. Jessie always wants everything in a big way. Especially money."

"Insider trading, Monique? Maybe buying shares in a high-tech DNA lab that's about to get a lot of attention?"

She reaches for her water bottle. It's empty. She pulls out the straw, drops it in the glass trash basket under her desk.

"PROHEMOGEN," Win then says. "DNA technology that genetically matches patients with drugs. The lab you picked for your media extravaganza may do ancestral profiles in criminal cases, but that's not where the money is."

She listens. She has that familiar look on her face when she is putting the case together.

"The money's in using genomics to help with the development of these next-generation superdrugs. Huge money, huge," Win says.

She doesn't answer, listens intently.

"The lab in California." He keeps going. "All the national attention you, the governor, will bring it because of this murdered old woman in Tennessee. Well, that's extremely helpful, now isn't it? You draw big attention to them and their lucrative biotechnology—give them that kind of free advertising—and guess what? Maybe their stock goes up. How much stock do you own?"

"That makes at least one thing obvious," she says. "Make it look as if I took the case home, was hiding it. But make sure it's found."

He looks at her for a long moment, says, "Pretty shrewd. Ruin you but save the day. The case file's found eventually. Publicity and more publicity. At your expense. Maybe the case is solved, maybe not, but a lot of publicity for that lab in California."

"It will get it anyway. Already is. The case is solved."

"The lab didn't do anything wrong. In fact, it did everything right. Helped solved the case."

She nods, distracted.

"Sad truth is, that murdered old woman didn't matter at all in any of this," Win says. "The powers that be didn't care."

Lamont is thinking, probably trying to move things along in a direction that suits her, says, "I know you probably don't believe me, but I did care. I wanted her case solved."

"How much stock do you own?" Win asks again.

"None."

"You sure?"

"That idea would never have entered my mind. I knew nothing about the company, but in Jessie's position, he's privy to all sorts of biotechnology, all sorts of private labs springing up all over the world. I didn't know about this, about the California lab and its biotechnology. I just thought we were working a twenty-year-old murder case that turned into a very public crime initiative I called At Risk. Really."

"Huber the one you were with the night before you were attacked? Probably when your keys disappeared? You said you were out, went to work straight from wherever it was you were staying."

Win has a minidisc running on top of her glass desk. He is taking notes.

"We had dinner. I can't . . . I can believe a lot of things about him. . . ."

"Motive." Win's not going to let her avoid the answer.

She takes her time, then, "Jessie and I are friends. Just as Jessie and you are friends."

"I seriously doubt it's quite the same."

"Earlier this year, he gave me some advice about my portfolio." She clears her throat, tries to steady her voice. "I made some money, realized what was going on a week later when I read in the paper that U.S. regulators had cleared the sale of a particular drug being developed at some lab, not the one in the Finlay case. Another one."

"Enough of a motive for him to set up your murder?"

"He's been getting insider tips in exchange for subcontracting out thousands of DNA kits to be analyzed for our database, for databases in other states based upon his recommendations. Major purchases of instruments for his labs, recommendations for other crime labs to buy the same things. It's been going on for years."

"He admitted all this to you?"

"After his stock advice, a lot of things began to add up." She glances at the recorder. "The more he told me, the more he implicated me. I'm guilty of insider trading. Next I'm guilty of conspiracy, of knowing what the director of the state crime labs is doing and I don't say a word. Not to mention . . ."

"Right. Your not-so-professional relationship."

"He loves me," she says with nothing in her voice as she stares at the recorder.

"Amazing way to show it."

"I ended it months ago, after he gave me the advice about the stock and I realized what he was into, what he had just gotten me into. What he is. I told him I didn't love him anymore, not that way."

"You threaten him?"

"I told him I wanted nothing more to do with his illegal activities, that they had to stop. And if they didn't, there would be consequences."

"You told him this when?"

"Last spring. Probably wasn't a smart thing to say," she mutters, staring hard at the recorder.

"You could have had a lawyer present,"

Win reminds her. "You said all this willingly. I didn't force you."

"Nice suit, by the way." She looks at his light gray suit, swallows, tries to smile.

"Emporio Armani, about three seasons out of date, seventy bucks. I didn't force you," he repeats.

"No, you didn't," she says. "And I'll take what comes."

"You'll testify against Huber?"

"It will be a pleasure."

Win picks up the recorder, pops out the disc, says, "Ever enter your mind you got enough glass in here to burn down your entire building?"

He selects a crystal paperweight, holds it up to the sun streaming through a window, focuses a white-hot dot on the disc. Lamont watches in amazement as a thin stream of smoke rises.

"What are you doing?" she says.

"You're living inside a tinderbox, Monique. Could burst into flames any minute. Maybe you should be more careful, take the heat off yourself, direct it elsewhere. Focus it very intensely where it belongs."

He hands her the ruined disc, their fingers lightly touching, says, "In case you get cold feet. Just pull this out and remember what I said."

She nods, tucks the ruined disc in a pocket.

"Another bit of advice. When someone else interviews you, like a grand jury, for example," he adds, "I suggest you leave out unnecessary details. The way I see it, most people are going to assume Huber was setting you up, conspiring with the governor, jealous, vindictive because you spurned him, greedy. On and on. I wrote down most of it. The relevant information." He holds up his notepad. "Just left out the misleading information. And you know what that information is. Such as any stocks Huber recommended, anything illegal he admitted to you that you never passed on. No proof. You could have chosen to make any investment you wanted, doesn't mean you got inside information, right? His word against yours."

She watches him, studies him, as he hits send on his cell phone.

"Sammy?" he says. "I want Huber brought in for questioning. Yup. The time has come. Get the warrant, we're going to search every place he owns. And our little buddy, Toby. Bring him in, too."

"With pleasure. Lay it on me," Sammy says.

"Attempted murder, conspiracy to murder, arson. And let's see." Win looks at Lamont, some of that old steely glint back in her eyes. "I'm sure the Feds will be delighted to hear all about his SEC violations."

"And then what? What about me?" Lamont asks Win as he ends the call. "You really think I'll be all right?"

"Funny how nothing changes," he says, getting up from his chair, smiling at her. "Funny how it's always about you, Monique."